BONES

Terrifying Tales
to HAUNT
Your DREAMS

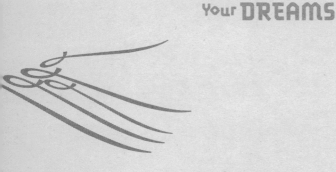

BONES

Terrifying Tales
to HAUNT
Your DREAMS

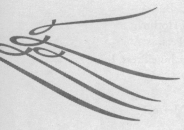

Edited by Lois Metzger

Scholastic Inc.

New York   Toronto   London   Auckland
Sydney   Mexico City   New Delhi   Hong Kong

No part of this publication may be reproduced, stored in a retrieval system, or transmitted in any form or by any means, electronic, mechanical, photocopying, recording, or otherwise, without written permission of the publisher. For information regarding permission, write to Scholastic Inc., Attention: Permissions Department, 557 Broadway, New York, NY 10012.

ISBN: 978-0-545-15891-6

© 2010 "YNK (You Never Know)" by Todd Strasser
© 2010 "The Skeleton Keeper" by David Levithan
© 2010 "In for a Penny" by Elizabeth C. Bunce
© 2010 "Growth Spurt" by Nina Kiriki Hoffman
© 2010 "Eyes on Imogene" by Richard Peck
© 2010 "The Three-Eyed Man" by Parachute Press, Inc.
© 2010 "Bones" by Margaret Mahy

Compilation copyright © 2010 by Lois Metzger
Foreword © 2010 by Lois Metzger

12 11 10 9 8 7 6 5 4 3 2 1   10 11 12 13 14 15/0

Printed in the U.S.A.
First printing, January 2010

CONTENTS

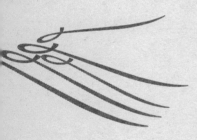

BONES

Terrifying Tales
to HAUNT
Your DREAMS

FOREWORD

Don't worry. The events in this book—no matter how frightening—never happened. Isn't it reassuring that nothing in these pages is real?

You won't be visited by a ghost who can't take his eyes off you, like the girl in Richard Peck's story, "Eyes on Imogene."

You'll never have to endure what Lizzie goes through in Elizabeth C. Bunce's "In for a Penny." Lizzie winds up in the same room as a hand of glory, which is the chopped-off hand of a hanged thief . . .

. . . who wants it back.

You can sleep soundly, unlike the boy in David Levithan's story, "The Skeleton Keeper." What's that eerie rattling inside his home every night? Why won't it leave him alone?

But if you can't sleep, it won't be because some long-dead person in a portrait comes calling on you, the way someone does to the boy in Margaret Mahy's story, "Bones."

You'll never meet up with a three-eyed man, as David does in R.L. Stine's "The Three-Eyed Man." David, of course, wants nothing to do with this man, but then David needs a favor. . . .

You may grow several inches in a summer, or go a couple of years without growing much at all. But you won't run across a strange woman with her own magic potion, which is what happens in "Growth Spurt" by Nina Kiriki Hoffman.

You can flip open a cell phone and it won't be haunted—like the phone in Todd Strasser's "YNK (You Never Know)." Next time you check to see if someone texted you, thank goodness there won't be bizarre messages about things none of your friends could possibly know.

But, while reading this book, you may begin to wonder . . .

What if the stories *are* real?

Why do they sound like actual events told by eyewitnesses?

Is that icy chill down the back of your neck trying to tell you something?

—Lois Metzger

YNK (YOU NEVER KNOW)

by Todd Strasser

"Let's have it, Johnny."

Two rows from Callie Jones's desk, Mr. Burton stood over Johnny Lin with his hand out.

"But I thought it was off, Mr. Burton," Johnny Lin pleaded. "I swear."

"Now!" Mr. Burton snapped angrily.

Johnny reached into his pocket and handed Mr. Burton his phone. The English teacher returned to the front of the classroom. "I am so tired of all of you fooling around with these phones in class. If you want this phone back, Johnny, have one of your parents come see me."

"B-b-but—" Johnny began to stammer, but quickly stopped when Mr. Burton furrowed his brow and glared at him.

Hands under her desk, Callie glanced at her friend Mandi in the back of the room and texted: **CSG** (Chuckle, Snicker, Grin).

A moment later, Callie's phone vibrated. She peeked down and saw: **SH^** (Shut Up!).

What? Callie thought, shocked by the reply. She twisted around and gave Mandi a brief, puzzled glance. *Why would she text that?*

"Callie?" Mr. Burton said sharply. "Is there something back there you find interesting?"

Callie quickly turned around and faced forward again. Later, after the period ended, she waited for Mandi in the hallway. "Why did you text me to shut up?" Callie asked.

Mandi scowled at her. "Did not."

"Did, too." Callie opened her phone and pointed at the screen. "It came from your phone."

"Well, I didn't send it, okay?" Mandi said.

"How can you say you didn't send it?" Callie asked, still pointing at the text message. "That's your number, and that means it came from your phone."

"Then the phone company's messed up, because I didn't send it," Mandi insisted. "Didn't you see what happened to Johnny? You'd have to be completely stupid to text in Burton's room." She headed into her next class.

Callie continued down the hall, totally annoyed with her friend. It was so obvious that Mandi had sent the text. Why wouldn't she just fess up?

Her next class was Spanish, with Ms. Arnold. As Callie entered the room, the Spanish teacher handed her a test sheet and said, "I hope you studied your vocabulary."

Callie gasped. She'd forgotten about the test! At her desk, she stared at the sheet and realized she knew hardly any of the answers.

Class began. All around her, kids scribbled on their sheets. Callie quietly took out her phone and held it behind her desk where Ms. Arnold couldn't see it. With one hand, she texted her friend David on the other side of the classroom: **CALIENTE?**

A moment later, she felt the phone vibrate. She pretended to yawn and glanced down at her lap. The text read: **DONT CHEAT!**

Callie couldn't believe it! Why were her friends being such jerks today? And it wasn't like she was really cheating. Normally she knew what *caliente* meant. She just couldn't remember at that moment. Next she texted her friend Alyssa, who was also in the class, and asked what the word meant.

The text that came back read: **MYOB** (Mind Your Own Business).

Callie felt like screaming. When she thought about all the times she'd helped her friends on their tests, it was unbelievable! She couldn't wait until class was over. As soon as she got out into the hall, she would give David and Alyssa a piece of her mind that they would never forget.

It wasn't long before class ended. Callie hadn't even bothered to finish the test. What was the point, when she knew hardly any of the answers? She'd failed, but so what? There'd be more tests that semester. As long as she passed the next few, she'd probably pass for the year. And, anyway, right now she was way more concerned about telling David and Alyssa a thing or two.

Callie handed in her test and headed for the door, but Gina Harmon stood in her path. Callie groaned inside. Gina was a loser with ratty hair and small reptilian teeth who wanted to be in Callie's crowd. The only times Callie and her friends let Gina hang around was when they could send her on errands to buy granola bars from the vending machine or get books they needed from the library.

But today, Gina was the last person in the world Callie wanted to see. The previous week, Gina had worn the cutest, brand-new pink rhinestone hoodie to school, and Callie asked if she could borrow it for the weekend. Of course Gina was thrilled to let Callie wear the hoodie, even though she'd made her promise to be careful with it because it had been a birthday present from her favorite aunt. Callie wore it to Brandi Calahan's birthday party on Saturday night (Gina wasn't invited) and stupid Grant Chimon managed to spill grape juice all over it.

The hoodie was completely ruined and it wasn't even Callie's fault! It was so unfair! Now, all week, Gina had been bothering Callie about bringing back the hoodie to school because her stupid aunt was coming to visit that weekend and would expect Gina to wear it.

"Hi, Callie. I hope you remembered my hoodie?" Gina asked.

"Oh, my gosh!" Callie pretended to gasp. "I'm so sorry! Can you believe I forgot it again?"

Gina's shoulders slumped with disappointment, and the corners of her mouth turned down. "This is the fourth day in a row you've forgotten. Tomorrow's Friday and my aunt's coming. You can't forget to bring it tomorrow. Promise?"

"I totally promise," Callie said, even though she knew she might have to pretend to be sick and stay home the next day, just to avoid Gina. And that wouldn't be easy, since she'd already missed way too many days that semester. "Gotta get to my next class. See ya later."

Callie got out of the classroom and looked for Alyssa and David.

She spotted them down at the end of the hall, talking and laughing with none other than Grant Chimon himself. *Perfect*, Callie thought as she marched toward them. *I'll tell off Alyssa and David for not helping me on the test, and I'll tell Grant that it's his fault that Gina's hoodie got ruined, and he'd better figure out how to replace it and fast.*

Just then she felt her phone vibrate. She flipped it open. The text message read: **DONT LIE.**

Callie stopped and frowned. *Lie?* she thought. Who had she lied to? She realized that it must have meant telling Gina she'd bring the hoodie to school tomorrow. But that wasn't really a lie, because losers like Gina didn't count.

Callie smirked to herself and started again toward her friends. Now she knew what was going on. They'd all gotten together to play a trick on her. They were sending her these stupid text messages and then pretending they weren't. As if their phones had minds of their own. Callie started walking faster, like she couldn't wait to get in their faces and tell them they were busted. But then she slowed down. She'd just had a better idea.

At lunchtime, Callie waited until she saw Gina enter the cafeteria. She made sure she "accidentally" got on the lunch line beside her.

"Oh, hi, Gina!" she said with a big smile.

Gina smiled back uncertainly. "Hi." It wasn't surprising that she was being wary, since the only other time Callie had acted friendly to her was when she wanted to borrow the pink hoodie.

"So, what looks good today?" Callie asked as they slid their trays down the rail.

"Nothing," Gina replied.

"Ha!" Callie pretended to laugh. "You're funny!"

Gina smiled sheepishly. "Well, it's true. Since when does anything they serve here ever look good?"

"True that," Callie agreed, as if Gina had just said the wisest and most profound thing ever. The cell phone in her pocket vibrated, and Callie flipped it open. The text read: **DONT B FONY!** Callie snapped the phone shut. She was beyond tired of her friends' jokes.

She and Gina paid the cashier and went into the cafeteria. Usually this would be an awkward moment, because Callie would walk toward the table where her friends sat, a table Gina had never been invited to.

"Want to sit with us?" Callie asked.

Gina's eyes widened with surprise. "Uh, sure!"

They headed for the table where Mandi, David, Alyssa, and Grant were already sitting. Callie was certain that Gina was thrilled. "Hey, guys, I asked Gina to sit with us today," Callie said, and sat down. Gina sat beside her. Both girls placed their backpacks on the floor.

"Oh, gosh!" Callie suddenly said. "I forgot to get silverware."

"I'll get it," Gina said, eager to be helpful and liked. She jumped up and headed back to the lunch line.

"Why'd you invite her to sit with us?" Alyssa whispered as soon as Gina was out of earshot.

"Why not?" Callie asked innocently. Meanwhile, she reached down to the outside pocket on Gina's backpack. "She's the only one here who hasn't pretended they didn't text me today."

Callie slid her hand into the pocket of the backpack and quietly took out Gina's phone. In the meantime, she felt her own phone start to vibrate, but she didn't bother to check it. She was sure it was from one of her friends, playing another trick on her.

"Would you get off that already?" Mandi said, annoyed. "I told you before, I didn't text you."

Callie looked at the others. "What about the rest of you?"

David, Alyssa, and Grant shook their heads.

Callie focused on David and Alyssa. "You guys didn't get a text from me during the Spanish test, asking what *caliente* meant?"

"No," Alyssa said.

David took out his phone and thumbed through his messages. He showed the list to Callie. "You didn't text me."

"So you erased it," Callie said. "What does that prove?"

Gina came back with the silverware, and everyone had lunch. Just before the period ended, while Callie was returning her tray to the kitchen, her cell phone vibrated. She opened it, knowing there'd be two messages—the one she hadn't checked at the table, and now a new one. The texts read: **DONT STEAL** and **DONT USE PEOPLE.**

Callie rolled her eyes and shook her head. She was *really* getting tired of this.

As if someone had heard her, Callie's phone didn't vibrate again for the rest of the school day. Neither did Gina's phone, because, after Callie took it, she turned it off and put it in her locker. Callie wasn't worried that Gina would discover that her phone was missing. Kids were always losing their phones. Usually if you waited a day or two, someone would find it and call you.

When school ended, Callie walked home with Gina's cell phone in her backpack. She had the perfect plan. Later that evening, she would text all her friends from Gina's phone, saying that she (Gina) was having a big party the next night and would pay everyone ten dollars each to attend. Callie was certain Gina would find out and be so embarrassed that she wouldn't dare set foot in school the next day. And then Callie wouldn't have to worry about bringing the hoodie.

It was early January and very cold. Icicles hung from the bare branches of the trees, and a thick white cloud came out with each breath Callie took. She listened to her iPod as she walked home. The streets and sidewalks were icy, and several times she started to slip and had to catch herself to keep from falling. When she got to her street, she saw an old lady taking bags of groceries out of her car. Callie had seen the woman before and knew she had a bad hip. She limped and winced in pain when she walked, and, in these icy conditions, she had to keep one hand on her car to brace herself. Callie saw that the back of her car was filled with bags of groceries. The old lady would have to make a lot of trips to get all those groceries inside.

Callie's cell phone vibrated. The message read: **B HLPFL.** She stopped and looked around. Somewhere, nearby, her friends had to be hiding behind a car or a tree and giggling. They must have followed her home. But Callie didn't care. It was a stupid trick and had gotten old really fast. She felt sorry for whoever was sending her these texts, because obviously they had nothing better to do with their time. Meanwhile, she had no intention of helping the old woman. She should have known that if she bought a lot of groceries, she'd have to make a lot of trips.

Callie continued down the sidewalk. Her house was on the next block, and, to get to it, she had to cross the intersection at the bottom of a hill. The intersection was always busy. She waited until the light turned green. As she stepped off the curb, the phone in her pocket vibrated. Callie flipped open the phone. The text read: **STOP!**

Callie stopped. Suddenly, a loud horn blared. A huge truck barreled down the hill, hit a patch of ice, and skidded right through the intersection.

The truck roared past, and the wind from it ruffled Callie's coat. The blood drained from her face, and she felt light-headed. Trembling, she turned and went back to the curb. If she had not stopped to read that text message, the truck would have run her over.

Still shaking, Callie looked around. One of her friends must have seen the truck coming and sent the text, right? But there was no one in sight. And even if they'd seen the truck coming down the hill, how could they have known it would hit the ice and skid? Once it had started to skid, there hadn't been nearly enough time for someone to compose and send a text. Callie felt a shiver, which wasn't caused by the cold. What if her friends had been telling the truth? What if they hadn't sent those texts?

She made sure the intersection was clear and crossed the street. While she continued toward home, the phone, clutched tightly in her hand, vibrated again. With trembling fingers, she flipped it open.

The message read: **THIS UR LAST CHANCE. FRM NOW ON, LISTN 2 WHAT I SAY!**

THE SKELETON KEEPER

by David Levithan

It killed me when Dad had to close up his office and bring all
the skeletons home. Our apartment was barely big enough for the
three of us, and now there were at least twenty more.

"No," my mom said. "*No.*"

But we didn't have a choice. Money was tight, and the future
looked even tighter if we didn't make "some big changes." My mom's
job behind a cash register didn't pay well. Because I was ten, the only
way I could make money was when neighbors needed something
done. And, if anything, the dead needed my dad's job more than
the living.

This was because my dad built skeletons. Real skeletons, from
real bones. When people died, they donated their bodies to science,
and then science donated their bones to my father, who put them
back together again. Then science would take them back—using
the skeletons as teaching tools, so future doctors could work with

real bones before operating on real people. But now, as other companies were making more accurate synthetic skeletons, fewer medical schools needed real ones. Or they skipped physical bones altogether and used computer simulations. My dad was being put out of business. But he was still receiving everyone's bones.

It had been my grandfather's job and my grandmother's job and my great-grandfather's job and my great-grandmother's job. So Dad wasn't letting go of it anytime soon. Even if it sent us to the poorhouse. Or killed us.

Dad brought the skeletons home one by one, each box neatly packed in the back of his station wagon, the closest to a coffin they'd ever come. Each of them had a name—not the real person's name, but a name he had given it. "Let's put Henry in the living room," he'd say. Or, "I have a feeling Loretta would be most at home in the laundry room." My mother would sigh and say, "Well, as long as Loretta doesn't block the dryer, that's fine."

There wasn't a workroom in our apartment, like there had been in Dad's office. If he wanted to make new skeletons, he'd have to use the dining-room table. Mom was not about to allow that.

"You have to be a salesman now," she told him. "Find some of these skeletons a home before you make any new ones."

I could see her point, even though I knew my father would go crazy if he couldn't get busy putting the skeletons together again soon. Meanwhile, our apartment was overrun by bones. Dad moved the couch a foot away from the wall so a row of skeletons could stand behind it. There were two in the kitchen closet, holding brooms and mops. There were four in my parents' bedroom, and the hallway was lined with skeletons, like a catacomb. There was even one (Charlie) that we kept in the shower, so if you wanted to use the shower, first you had to move him behind the door.

The laundry room was the spookiest because that's where the incomplete skeletons went. Loretta was missing her jaw, a leg, and a few ribs. Bailey had no fingers and no toes. Lefty only had a left side; no one knew what had happened to the right.

I should have been used to all this. Skeletons had been a part of my life since the day I was born. There were even baby pictures with me posed in the lap of my grandparents' favorite skeleton, Noel, who ended up in a classroom at Harvard Medical School. For as long as I could remember, my parents had taught me that bones were nothing to be afraid of.

"We all have them," Dad would point out. "Just because they're hidden doesn't mean they're scary."

By the time I was seven, I could name most of the 206 bones in the body. And I had touched most, if not all, of these 206 bones in my dad's workshop. I thought I was all right with bones. And I was.

Until they came to live with me.

My mom had told my dad there was no way she was going to allow any skeletons in my bedroom. But I knew Dad still needed space, and I didn't think it would be a problem to share a room with a few. So I carried on until Mom relented—and Clark, Ingrid, and Montgomery came to stay with me.

Big mistake.

During the day, it wasn't much of a problem. My room was pretty small, but I could usually maneuver myself around the skeletons when I needed something from my closet (which Clark and Ingrid blocked) or wanted to open my window (which Montgomery guarded).

The worst was at night.

My room was on the first floor, and every time a car would pass, the edges of the headlight beams would shift into my room. I would be lying in bed, trying to sleep, and for a moment the walls and ceilings would be scanned by a dim wave of light. I had grown used to this . . . but not with the skeletons around. Suddenly, I was beset by the scariest shadows I'd ever seen. Right there—on my walls, on my ceiling—it was like the bones were coming to life. *It's only bones*, I told myself. *It's only Clark and Ingrid and Montgomery.*

As if by giving them names, they could be my friends.

As if skeletons could be my friends.

The first night, I eventually tired myself out and went to sleep. The second night was harder, and the third night was harder still.

The fourth night was when I started to hear the rattling.

It wasn't coming from Clark or Ingrid or Montgomery. It wasn't coming from anywhere in my room. At first I thought it might be a car out on the road. Or someone moving furniture upstairs. But it went on and on.

Rattle. Rattle. Rattle.

Somewhere beyond the room. Bones shifting. Bones knocking into each other. Shaking.

I tried to ignore it. I tried to play songs in my head, tried to think of other things.

But, as I did that, something strange began to happen.

Lying there in my bed, I started to feel like I myself was a skeleton.

Like I myself was made entirely of bones and nothing else.

Imagine your body without any softness. Imagine the hard bones in the night air. Imagine the weight of movement. Imagine no longer breathing.

That's what it felt like.

I didn't sleep at all that night—not until school the next day, when Mrs. Cantor caught me with my eyes closed. My best friend, Simeon, made fun of me for that. I knew I couldn't tell him about the sound, or about feeling like I was a skeleton. But I did tell him my dad had moved his skeletons to our house.

Naturally, Simeon wanted to come over and see.

I couldn't really say no. Simeon's mom worked in an art gallery, and, every now and then, she'd have to take something home for safekeeping. Simeon would tell me about it, and we'd sneak into her room to take a look. Sometimes it was a painting, and sometimes it would be something really odd that somebody was buying for a fortune—like a larger-than-life-size hamburger made out of thousands of paper clips.

Simeon wasn't disappointed. We'd been friends for a while, so he'd seen some of my dad's skeletons before. But never this many, and never in my house.

"You should invite more people over," Simeon told me. "Charge admission. You could make some easy money."

"I don't think so," I said. My father had always been clear with me: These skeletons were for science, not show. Numerous times over the years, he had been approached by "collectors"—rich people who thought it would be cool to have the skeleton of somebody else to decorate their mansion, or to be a prop at their expensive Halloween party, or (for all we knew) to become a human chew toy for a beloved poodle. My dad, like my grandparents and my great-grandparents before him, always said no.

"These people trusted us with their bones," he would tell me. "We have to honor that trust."

I could see that Simeon was going to argue with me, but then Dad came home from a meeting with one of his clients, looking grimmer than usual. Simeon said a quick good-bye, and my father retreated to the laundry room until dinner.

At some point, my mom must have come home and gone into the laundry room to talk to him, because by the time I got to the kitchen, they were in the middle of an argument.

"You're a victim of your own success," she was telling him. "The skeletons you build last too long, so the schools don't need new ones. What you need are some really clumsy medical students to wreck the ones they already have."

My father flinched at that. Seeing this, Mom went over and put her arms around him, hugging him so her chin nestled into his shoulder.

"I'm sorry," she said. "It's just a joke. I'm trying to think of other possibilities. But there aren't any more shifts for me at work—everyone needs the extra hours nowadays. I'm sure we'll think of something."

Dad shook his head. "I really wasn't expecting them to say no today."

"Times are tough all over," my mother said. "Except for really rich people."

We didn't talk about it again at dinner, and I tried not to think about it for the rest of the night, but trying not to think about it was as pointless as trying not to think about how I was made of bones. Everything I touched—I imagined the bones beneath my fingers. Every time I breathed—I imagined my lungs pressing against my ribs.

It was even worse that night. The rattling was louder, more beseeching. It wasn't coming from my parents' room—no, they were asleep. And it wasn't coming from outside the window. It was coming from another part of the apartment.

I tried to block out the sound. I couldn't. I tried to remind myself I wasn't bones—I was skin, I was muscle, I was blood.

But it was bone I felt.

About three in the morning, I finally got out of bed. I had to find out where the rattling was coming from.

I didn't turn on the lights. I didn't want to wake my parents. So when I tried to guide myself down the hallway, it was like being in a maze of bones. As I walked through the dark, I touched skulls, arms, ribs, fingers. Silent bones. Watching bones. A forest of bones, with the rattling in front of me. The pulse of bones. Beating. Beating. Beating.

Finally, I got to the laundry room.

It was coming from behind the door.

Louder.

Louder.

I knew I just had to open the door. I had to go inside. But I couldn't. It was like the door itself was a breastbone, guarding a heart. And it wasn't going to let me through. Instead, I would be tortured by the sound. Tortured, until I could figure out how to make it stop.

That night, I wanted to sleep like the dead. But instead I lay awake.

No way to shut my eyes.

No way to shut my ears.

No way to scream.

At school, Simeon was relentless.

"Five dollars a person," he told me. "Twenty people at a time. Fifteen minutes. That's a hundred dollars for fifteen minutes."

I told him no.

He asked again.

I told him no.

He asked again.

I told him why.

"Think of it as a science field trip," he said.

When he put it like that, it didn't seem so wrong. Dad and Mom were both always talking about how people needed to see what their bodies were made of, so they wouldn't be scared of them and would instead understand what "incredible machines" we were.

A science field trip.

A hundred dollars for fifteen minutes.

My best friend.

I told him yes.

We had to wait a few days before giving the tour. My mother

wasn't the problem—she was working long hours and usually got home just before dinner. It was my dad who got in the way; he was home all the time, like a ghost wandering aimlessly through the place where he had once lived. He tinkered a little with the incomplete skeletons in the laundry room, but mostly he dusted the other ones, making them as presentable as possible, as if at any moment a scientist might ring the doorbell and say he wanted to buy the whole lot. Which, of course, never happened. Word had gotten out about my father's predicament, and every now and then he'd get a call about his "inventory." But these weren't scientists calling. These were collectors. Dad was always polite with them, but he always said no and looked sad after he hung up.

Finally, he mentioned that he was going to be meeting with my uncle for lunch on Friday. Our school happened to have a half-day, but I didn't tell him that. Instead, I told Simeon to line up the twenty kids for our fifteen-minute field trip.

That night the rattling sounded like it was coming from the house itself. Every wall was a bone. Every piece of furniture was a bone. And they were all quaking, all knocking against each other.

I ran fast through the hallway. I knocked down one of the skeletons but didn't think about it. I threw myself at the door.

This time, it opened.

I was in the laundry room. The dark laundry room.

The washer was off. The dryer was off.

But the noise of bones was in my ears.

The next morning, Friday morning, my mother came into my

room before she left for work. "What happened?" she asked. At first I thought she knew about everything. But then she went on: "One of the skeletons was knocked over last night. Dad's fixing it right now. Were you wandering around? You have to turn the lights on, sweetie." She sighed, looking even sadder than I'd seen her recently. "It's much too dangerous in the dark."

It's much too dangerous in the dark.

She had no idea.

In the end, Simeon got twelve kids to come to my apartment, not twenty. Still, it was sixty dollars.

Right away, things started going wrong. We'd told them not to touch anything, but they couldn't help daring each other to touch *everything*. Marley (the person) got caught in John (the skeleton) and nearly knocked three skeletons over trying to get out. I couldn't watch everyone at once, so I'd be trying to tell Eddie in my bedroom not to shake Clark's hand, and then I'd hear a scream from the laundry room and see that Michael had turned off the lights and closed the door on two girls in our class, Ashley and Hannah, trapping them inside.

"This has to stop!" I yelled to Simeon. But he looked helpless, too.

And then my dad came home.

He was early, and he had my uncle with him. The minute he opened the door, he knew what was going on. *Everyone* knew what was going on. Suddenly, kids were darting out of the apartment. Simeon shot me a sorry glance and went with them.

"How could you do this?" Dad asked.

I was trying to find the words to explain. Then Michael came up, looking snotty.

"I want my money back," he demanded.

Simeon had the money. I didn't.

With the most disappointed look I've ever seen, my father asked Michael, "How much?"

"Five dollars," Michael said. At least he didn't lie.

My father took out his wallet and paid Michael five dollars.

I wanted to disappear. I wasn't worthy of bones—or skin or breath.

"Go to your room," my father said.

I did. But, even from there, I could hear him and Uncle Ron arguing.

"You see—even your kid is desperate!" Uncle Ron shouted.

I couldn't hear my father's reply. But Uncle Ron wouldn't let up: "The answer to everything is in that box, Greg. All you have to do is put it together and sell it. Just one. Legally, the bones are yours. You got them fair and square. People would pay a lot of money for them, and you know that."

My father kicked him out of the house. Then he shut himself in the laundry room. He didn't even check to see if my "tour" had done any damage.

That was left to me.

That night I found it.

The source of the rattling.

The box.

I'd heard what my uncle had said, and now I knew what to look for. Not for a skeleton, but for a box. A box of bones.

It was hidden behind the water heater. A wooden box.

As soon as I touched it, the rattling stopped.

As if now that I had finally found it, it didn't need to call to me.

Carefully, I opened the lid. Quietly, I took out the first bones. A finger. Exactly the size of my finger.

Then a tibia. Exactly the size of my tibia.

A skull. Exactly the size of my skull.

There wasn't much room on the floor of the laundry room, but I laid it all out. The skeleton of a boy, all ready to be assembled. Every single bone, 206 of them, was there.

I stood over the skeleton like it was my X-ray shadow. I hooked together the foot and put it up against my own foot. The exact same size. Then I picked up the skull and stared into the empty eye sockets.

"Tell me what to do," I whispered.

And I got an idea.

The next day, I called my uncle. I told him what I'd found. I didn't tell him what I was going to do. I wanted to make sure I had the right box. He said I did. He said he knew people who would pay big money for it.

"That kid was famous," he said. "They called him the 'million-dollar boy'—you know how they say some kids are gifted? Well, it was like he got the biggest gift of all. The things he could create when he was just six—it was incredible. You weren't born yet, so you wouldn't remember. And then, one day, his brain just fails on him.

He was about your age. People couldn't believe it. And then everyone wanted to know what made him tick. Not just the scientists—obviously, the family was okay with scientists checking him out. But all the rich people who'd bought his stuff . . . they wanted more. Rumor has it that one of his nannies smuggled out a few of his drawings from his playroom and made a fortune."

I didn't want to hear any more. At least now I knew for sure where my idea had come from.

He was still creating, through me.

I got my sixty dollars from Simeon and went to the store to buy supplies.

I knew it was risky. Even though I was dying to get out of bed, I had to wait at least an hour until my parents' last sounds of the night. Then I tiptoed through the darkness. This time, the skeletons in the hallway kept their distance.

I went into the laundry room, closed the door, and worked all night, until daybreak. Also the next night. And the night after that. During the day, I kept what I was doing well hidden—in the closet of my room.

Was I betraying my father? My grandparents? My great-grandparents?

Would they understand?

It took four nights before I was finished. Everything my father had taught me, I put into it. I didn't know if he'd be proud or if it would destroy him.

I took pictures of what I'd done and sent the pictures to the right people, recommended by Simeon's mom. I waited for a response and got one immediately.

We will pay you, the response said. *We will pay you a lot.*

The hitch was: In order to receive the money, my parents had to know about it. I was too young to be paid. So I had to tell them.

I waited until my mother got home. I waited until my father emerged from his bedroom, where he'd been lightly polishing Betsy.

"I have something to show you," I said.

I had put it in the middle of my room, right in front of the bed. I led my parents to the door and opened it. They didn't even come inside. They just stood in the doorway and stared.

I watched my father's expression.

Surprise.

Confusion.

Shock.

"What is that?" he asked. Then, "*Who* is that?"

But he had to know. It was the boy from the box.

Only . . . it wasn't.

"How did you . . . ?" my father said.

"You taught me," I said quietly. "You taught me the bones."

My mother just stared.

"They'll pay me fifty thousand dollars for it," I told them.

"But what is it?" my father asked again.

"It's art," I said.

I had put together the boy's skeleton—not the real skeleton but a second one, duplicated in blue clay. Because I knew bones, I could do it. It looked real.

"Do you have any idea who that is?" my father asked, looking at me for the first time.

"Uncle Ron told me. But I didn't tell anyone else. No one will ever know. His bones are safe and his story is safe."

I could tell from the look on my father's face that he, too, would keep this secret. Because I knew, too, that he realized the idea hadn't come from me. It had come from the bones.

"The bones trust you," my father would say. "And you should trust the bones."

I do, Dad.

I do.

IN FOR A PENNY

by Elizabeth C. Bunce

If you come into the Red Drake Inn on a rainy night and ask for a table by the fire, don't be surprised if they have one open. The Red Drake's a big inn, and prosperous—probably the biggest on the Haymarket Road. But even on a crowded night, when the wind shrieks past the gables, and rain whips sideways 'cross the moon, and the dogs are restless, the table by the fireplace is usually empty.

So when the hostess leads you there, sits you down, and asks you what's your pleasure, and you run your hand across the worn wooden top, with all its glass rings and burn marks from hot plates, and your fingers come to the big deep gash in the wood—don't be surprised if you feel a little chill or notice the regulars trying hard not to stare at you. And don't be surprised about the silence that falls, or that it takes the serving girl a powerful long time to bring your food. . . . Because that's the table where Lizzie Penny won her fight with a ghost.

Twelve-year-old Lizzie was a maid-of-all-work, helping out in the kitchen, and the public room, and the guest rooms—and Red Drake folk said she was steady and dependable, for all she was a Penny. That night, though, she wasn't feeling quite so steady.

It was the end of winter, when things are trying to come back from the dead—a cold, hard, ugly, flat sort of day that slipped into evening far too early. Lizzie was out in the yard, rounding up the chickens and trying to shush out of her mind the fool story Jem had told her about "henny-haunts" that come after girls who steal their eggs. Everyone knew that if you scribed a big black circle round the henhouse, it kept the birds safe from haunts, and a big black dog in the yard kept them safe from foxes. Still, the fading light made the coop look all funny-like, and Lizzie was glad to empty her bowl of grain and head back into the warm, lamplit inn.

"*Hsst!* Lizzie-girl!"

She started, nearly dropping the bowl. Her brother, Jem, crouched in the shadows by the stable door. Jem was a typical, no-account Penny—lazy and shiftless, with no honest work behind or before him. Lizzie liked to hold her head up high and pretend she didn't know him, but that was harder to do when it was your pa wavin' at you from the side of the barn. With a sigh, she set the bowl down and went to see what they wanted.

What they wanted was to rob the Royal Mail, the big stagecoach coming through that night with all kinds of money and valuables aboard. Stages stopped at the Red Drake all the time, and her pa and brother were always trying to think of a way to "lighten their loads." So far they hadn't succeeded, and Lizzie just shrugged.

"Now, don't you go all high-and-mighty on me, girl! Why do

you think we got you this job here at the inn?" Pa leaned in close. "I've got a pretty trick up my sleeve tonight. Meet us here at midnight and be sure to leave the doors unlocked."

Lizzie flinched from Pa's hand on her arm. "But Seth will be sleeping on the hearth, and the Drakes' room is right above the street. How will you get into the inn without them noticing?"

"I reckon Pa's got it all planned out," Jem said, his face cracking into a sneer. "Says them birds'll sleep like babies while we just slip in and grab all the eggs we can carry, if you take my meaning."

Lizzie was all too sure she did, and she couldn't stop the thread of worry creeping up the back of her dress that evening as she went about her chores. Just a few weeks earlier, the Penny gang had had a close shave at the brewery, and one of the men had been caught and hanged—a man called Bert Lively, whom Lizzie had known all her life. She could remember Bert whittling by their fire, or teasing her for her curly hair. They said his body hung at the old crossroads a whole fortnight before somebody finally cut him down.

That night, when the fires in the common room burned down, and Seth the kitchen boy curled up on the hearth, Lizzie stood at her window, watching the moonlit roadway. The Royal Mail had rolled in late, blue and gold and glossy, looking very official. They said the driver carried a pair of ivory-handled pistols—she knew he carried a whip. Surely he could protect himself from highwaymen; how did Pa think he could pull off such a plan?

Pa and Jem and three other men showed up about a quarter 'til midnight, jostling and snickering and trying hard to keep to the shadows, but making far too much noise about it. Her belly like a hunk of lead, Lizzie crept downstairs, slipping past Seth with his gentle snores, and swung the inn doors open to admit the thieves.

They came in, all riled up and nerves ajangle. Lizzie hung back in the shadows by the kitchen, hoping hard that somebody upstairs would hear the racket, come down, and scare everybody away.

"Quiet!" Pa's voice, normally thin as wire, came down like a thunderclap. Lizzie jumped—so did Jem and the others, but they hushed. Seth stirred on the hearth, but that was all. Pa glared at everyone as he took a filthy feed sack from under his baggy coat.

"Look close, lads," he said as he reached into the sack. "Our luck is changing—right here and now, tonight." He drew out an odd, misshapen sort of thing—cold, gray, and wax-stiff. Lizzie drew in her breath. It was a man's hand, which Pa upended on the tabletop close to the fireplace. The hand sat there, palm up, like it was waiting for somebody to give it something.

"Pa!" Her voice came unbidden, shrill and strained. In the flickering firelight, the hand seemed to twitch—but that couldn't be. It was dead, dead and preserved, like the stuffed stag's head above the fireplace.

Only not a bit like that at all.

She knew what it was, of course, for all she'd never seen one. It went by different names—*hand of glory, five-finger light, hangman's candle*. The hand of a hanged thief, cut from his corpse by moonlight and made into a candlestick, was a sort of thieves' good-luck charm—something the men joked and dreamed about: yearning tales of all they could steal, if they ever got hold of such a prize.

And now her pa had one.

"Pa . . ." Lizzie's voice was low and warning, but Pa ignored her. Out of the sack he took a candle, low and fat and ill-formed.

It looked like a normal candle, but Lizzie knew how candles were made—from an animal's rendered fat—and felt the shiver overtake her.

Pa settled the candle in the hand's palm and struck a match to light it.

All at once, the other lights in the room went out. With a *whoosh!* the fire in the grate went out, and the inn's common room fell into darkness, except for the awful, wavering light of the candle held by the dead man's hand.

Jem let out a shrill, cackling laugh that made the hairs on Lizzie's arms stand on end. "Hush!" she said, waving him to silence. But Pa's face broke into a slow grin as he watched the peaceful form of Seth the kitchen boy sound asleep on the cold hearth. Lizzie followed Pa's gaze and stared.

"Nothing'll wake him now, girl. Long as that candle burns, every soul in this house'll sleep the sleep of the dead." To prove it, Pa gave one of the benches a hard shove. It banged against the stone floor so loudly that Lizzie thought she'd come out of her skin. But after she held her breath a piece, nobody came running downstairs.

The men whooped and hollered their way round the common room, kicking benches and slamming down pitchers, until Pa yelled for silence. "The folk in *here* can't hear us, lackwits, but the charm only works *inside* the inn. Last thing we need is for some busybody to come walking by and sound the alarm. Now let's move. Tom, Dick, Sowerby—you lot check the pickings in the guest rooms. Jem and me'll hit the stables. Lizzie-girl, you're our lookout. Got it? Don't let nobody through those doors, and mind any drafts on that candle flame."

Off they went, creeping through the dark corners of the inn, bumbling and laughing through the blackness. Somehow it was eerier—all of them making so much noise, and not a bit caring that somebody might hear.

Lizzie hunched into her shawl and set up watch near the door, shut tight against the night. With the fire out, it was darker than dark in the common room, and every shadow that leaped and swayed made her heart jump. Outside, the night wind was building up, a shrill whistle twisting at the corners of the old inn, rattling the doors and shutters. The lights were on at the printer's shop 'cross the way, and she felt reassured knowing that some folk were awake and close by.

Behind her, the *thing* on the table sent up its weird flickering light, cold and blue and uncanny. She knew it would keep burning until one of the thieves put it out, and, until then, everyone in the house would stay fast asleep. Only the guilty could stay awake while it burned. Lizzie scowled—why should it count *her* among that rotten number? It didn't seem rightly fair.

Vexed, she hopped off her bench, squared her shoulders, and walked straight over to the table. She and that thing would have a talking-to. After all, she was Lizzie Penny, inn girl at the Red Drake. She'd caught rats in the larder, dispatched hens with the big axe just outside the barn door, even chased an angry dog away from the yard. No daft charm from any ghost story would get the best of her.

The hand just lay there, a cold waxen lump, aglow in a light like Lizzie'd never seen. Candles were supposed to burn yellow and bright and friendly—cozy cheer against shadows and the things that lurked in them. She was about to blow 'cross the flame and puff it out for good, when she heard the sound of footsteps.

She tensed. Of course, there were footsteps inside the inn, with all the men banging about upstairs—but these were distant and strange, almost more a feeling than a sound. Somebody outside, coming toward the inn? She scurried to the window, peered out, and saw a man shambling down the street, back by the milliner's shop. The man wouldn't hear them from outside, not with the wind howling so.

Then why had she heard him?

The man was already that much closer, down to the chandler's and the stationer's. That wasn't right; how had he come so far, so fast?

Lizzie sucked in her breath. Hadn't the lights been *on* at the hatmaker's shop just a moment ago? Fine chance that they doused the light just when this fellow was walking past.

The sounds of the men upstairs seemed to fade away. She barely heard them, popping doors and stumbling over loose floorboards. But the man outside, with his too-quick-to-see footsteps, was closer now. Something was strange about him, one arm shoved into his coat pocket like that. Something familiar, too—did she know him? One of the regulars, come for a late-night pint?

Now *that* was odd—the lights at the printer's going out, just then. Where was Pa? Surely it didn't take so long to rustle through the stables.

The man paused at the door to the Red Drake. He banged on the wood, three slow knocks that rumbled through Lizzie's bones.

Thump. Thump. Thump.

Pa's words came back: *Don't let nobody in.* She crouched below the window frame so he wouldn't see her if he looked in.

Thump.

Thump.

"Pa . . ." Her own voice, soft and uncertain. Where were they?

Thump.

Cold candlelight washed the room, and silence pressed in all around. Why couldn't she hear the men upstairs?

A face peered in the window. She could make out his features a bit—why did he look so strange? Slowly, Lizzie rose from the floor, until she stood face-to-face with the man outside—and recognized him.

Bert Lively. The same Bert Lively who was dead and hanged, buried these three weeks in the boneyard. Lizzie stumbled backward against a table.

He didn't seem to see her—just thumped again at the door, and then, when it didn't open, came on in anyway.

Lizzie couldn't move. Bert Lively had stepped through the heavy oak doors like they were made of mist, and now stood in the common room with Lizzie.

She thought she should scream, but her voice wouldn't come.

Bert took no notice of her, just made his way across the common room, walking *through* tables and benches, like he knew what he'd come for and wouldn't be denied. He cast a sly glance around the room, then reached across the bar to where Mistress Drake kept the strongbox. For a moment, Lizzie thought his sleeve was too long—and then she realized why.

Bert's arm had no hand on it.

Lizzie squeaked—just a tiny bubble of fear, no bigger than a mouse rustle. Bert swung his pale head in her direction—and that was enough for Lizzie. She bolted out of that common room like the law was on her tail.

Her footsteps banged on the floor; she slammed doors open and shut—but nobody came running. "Pa! Pa! Jem!" she cried, flying across the cobbled inn yard, past the snug chicken coop and the sleeping watchdog, toward the barn. She hit the barn doors, tripping on the threshold and tangling her feet in the axe handle. Stumbling through the darkened barn, she hollered to wake the dead, but her voice met only silence.

And out there in the night with her was dead Bert Lively, up and walking around and wanting things he had no need for anymore.

Lizzie's voice rose to a shriek, but not even the chickens stirred. And then she discovered why, when she tripped the second time— over the slumped, snoring form of Jem, propped against the blue side of the Royal Mail stagecoach, right beside Pa, who was fast asleep with his hand still on the coach door.

"Pa!" Lizzie screamed, shaking him, kicking at Jem's shins— but neither stirred. "Pa!" The charm was supposed to work only on people who *lived* in the house—but somehow, something had gone wrong.

And the hand's owner coming back to claim his share of the loot? That was *plenty* wrong, indeed.

Outside, the wind shrieked over the gables. With a chill, Lizzie wondered if the sound *wasn't* the wind. She found herself slowly crossing the yard, trying to work out why things had taken such a strange turn. Maybe it was because Bert Lively was a thief himself and couldn't resist one last job—even from beyond the grave. But then, why had the robbers fallen asleep, too?

Maybe Bert was after something more than just what was in the cash box.

When Lizzie returned to the common room, she discovered what that something was. Bert stood at the table trying to pry up the hand—*his* hand. But his ghostly arms kept passing right through it. The mad howling came from him every time he reached for the hand but came up short.

Lizzie stared, transfixed, until a cold thought wormed its way into her mind. *What would happen if Bert got his hand back?*

Lizzie didn't want to find out.

She'd heard that you had to speak strongly to haunts, give 'em what for. She took a deep breath. "Bert!" Her voice was sharp and nervous. "Bert, you're dead. You won't be needin' that anymore. Get on back up to the boneyard."

Her words sounded foolish, and Bert paid her no mind. Was he succeeding? His other hand seemed to catch somehow, in the flesh of the hand, as it passed through. Not like light or mist anymore, but like water.

"Bert, that ain't yours no longer." Lizzie crept closer. "Now leave off."

Bert's cries grew louder. He flailed uselessly at the hand and its candle on the table, still burning its eerie glow. Maybe if the light was out . . . ?

Lizzie took three bold steps straight up to the thing and, dodging out of the way of Bert's hazy arms, blew hard on the candle flame.

Nothing happened. The light didn't go out. Again and again she blew, but the little blue flame wouldn't die. Frantic now, she did as Bert did—grabbed at the hand on the table, wanting to fling the whole thing into the fire. But though her fingers grasped the cold, dead flesh, the candle wouldn't budge. The hand was stuck fast to the table, as if bolted down.

She yanked hard at the hand again, and the whole table moved. A strangled cry filled the common room, and this time Lizzie wasn't sure it came from Bert. She let go of the hand and stumbled back toward the hearth, nearly falling over the still-sleeping Seth. Bert tried again to grab hold of the hand—were the fingers holding the candle *twitching*?

Lizzie scrabbled to her feet. Skirts flying, she flung back 'cross the inn yard and fetched the axe by the barn door. It was heavy in her hands, solid and comforting. She hauled it back to the common room, where Bert now had a grip on the hand. Trying to pull it up from the table, his stump curved round it, drawing it toward his chest.

"Bert Lively, I said *get on back*!" Lizzie heaved the axe upward and, throwing all her weight into it, brought it down hard on the table. It smashed clean through the hand, splitting it in two. One half flew straight into the fireplace, where the candle bounced into the embers. The other half skittered across the floor like a spider, running on little finger feet.

Bert lurched after his fleeing fingers, chasing them into a corner. Lizzie's palms were sweaty, and the axe wouldn't budge, caught solid in the wood tabletop.

Behind her, Lizzie heard something stir. The candle in the fireplace sputtered in a pool of melted tallow, its flame dancing into nothingness. Across the room, Bert still tried to catch his fingers.

But with every wild grab, his form grew harder and harder to see. His shrieking wail was fading to a soft moan, until Lizzie couldn't tell it apart from the wind.

"Bert . . . ?" Lizzie crept closer, but poor Bert Lively was no more than a wisp of smoke, grasping at a lump of bones and wax on the floor. As she watched, he reached out his handless arm one last time—and faded into the night.

"Lizzie? What's going on?" Seth sat up and rubbed his face, blinking at the axe still buried in the upturned table. "What happened?"

Lizzie stared round the common room. Except for the disarray of tables and benches scattered everywhere—and the heavy thumping of her heart—everything was normal. She could hear the inn coming back to life—odd bumps and muffled oaths as the sleeping thieves roused themselves. She took a deep breath. Stooping to right the table and free the axe, she shrugged.

"A rat" was all she said.

Long afterward, folk told the story of Lizzie and her ghost, and how she saved the Red Drake twice over that night—from haunts *and* thieves. It's hard to say who told them the tale, though, since Lizzie wasn't the sort to spread tales or spin a tall yarn.

It might have been Pa; he always liked to boast about an adventure, whether he'd taken part or not. He'd no doubt have had a thing or two to say about how his Lizzie convinced the Drakes that the Penny gang had just gotten lost trying to find lodgings for the night. People did wonder, though, about the way Lizzie's pa would always pull his sleeve down low and rub his wrist, like a nervous habit.

Still, that gash in the tabletop was real as real, and Red Drake folk had to admit they slept uncommonly fine the night the Royal Mail came through. And it did seem strange how, soon afterward, Jem Penny went and got himself honest work as a field hand up Trawney way. Loose tongues had lots to say on the matter, all over town. But Lizzie, she'd just smile and heft that axe over her shoulder, like an old friend.

GROWTH SPURT

by Nina Kiriki Hoffman

When my best friend, Reed, came home after a summer on the East Coast with the other half of his family, he was six inches taller. We were both about to start seventh grade, and it wasn't fair. I hadn't grown at all that summer. Reed had spent the summer with his cousins—hiking, canoeing, and riding horses. I spent the summer reading manga, playing video games, and going to early showings of second-run movies, which only cost a dollar. Guess who ended up with muscles and a tan.

I saw Reed exactly one time before our first day of school. I had called him as soon as he had gotten back home, to ask how his summer went and when we could get together—there was an early show of *Bloodzilla* the next day, probably our last chance to see a movie on a weekday.

He told me about the outdoor life he'd been leading, but even then I couldn't imagine how much he'd changed.

"I don't have time for a movie, Mike," he said. "Mom has to buy me new clothes for school. But I'll ask her to break for lunch at the mall's food court. Meet you there around noon?"

The mall was full of kids and parents shopping for school stuff. I saw a million kids I knew who didn't know me back. I'd always been more of a watcher than a joiner; at least that was what I told myself when nobody except Reed joined me for anything.

I didn't recognize Reed. If I hadn't noticed his mom, I would have walked right by him.

"Hey, Mikey," Reed said as I approached their table. People had called me Mikey before, but Reed never had. I hated that nickname and he knew it. He stood up and up and up, and looked down at me with a big smile, his teeth white against his tan. He looked like he'd changed species.

"Hi, Mrs. Tedesco. Hi, Reed. How was your summer?" I said.

"Better than yours, looks like," replied Reed. Another flashy smile.

I wondered if my old friend was still inside this new Reed package. I'd been waiting all summer for him to get home, and now—

"Knock knock," I said, my ready-made escape for all occasions.

Reed sighed. "Who's there?"

"Carlotta."

"Carlotta who?"

"Car gotta lotta steam. I gotta go," I said, waved at him, and ran. Okay, not one of my better efforts, but I hadn't known ahead of time I'd need a good knock-knock joke for a quick getaway.

* * *

Mom had taken me to the mall two weeks earlier. She's a great one for wanting to get things done before everybody else. She hates crowds and noise.

So I already had my new school clothes. But clothes weren't my problem. Reed was my problem. First day of school, there he was, taller than most of the guys our age, although two girls had gotten tall over the summer, too. The tall girls were on the fringe of the crowd around Reed. He was laughing and joking with a bunch of people we never talked to. The stuck-up people who had called us nerds and losers the year before.

Nope, I decided my old friend Reed was nowhere inside that package anymore. I hitched up my backpack, pulled up my hood, and eased past them.

With school started, I knew I'd see a lot of Reed because we were taking all the same classes. I couldn't avoid him if he wanted to talk to me.

He didn't.

It was my worst first day of school since first grade. (I didn't meet Reed until the second day of first grade—he'd been sick that first day.)

On the way home, I skipped my usual route down Grace Street, the one Reed and I had walked all last year, where we stopped at the library and went to the 7-Eleven. Instead, I went down Burns, and that was when I saw the sign over a narrow brown door squashed between two brightly lighted antique shops.

FORTUNES TOLD
PROBLEMS SOLVED
IDEAS HATCHED

It could be just what I needed!

I peeked through the door's window. All I saw inside was a narrow green staircase with two brown walls on either side. A small sign on the door read:

COME IN AND COME UP

I opened the door and heard a jingly wind-chime sound. Some kind of incense smell, like a forest, puffed out as I stepped inside.

This was so dumb. I should just go home and live with the fact that I'd lost my best friend and would never find another. I could watch the world go by. I already knew I was good at that.

"Close the door," someone yelled from upstairs. The voice wasn't high or low, somewhere in the middle, and it made me think of butterscotch.

"Huh?" I said.

"Come in or go out. Either way, close the door."

I gripped the doorknob, ready to leave. Instead, I shut the door behind me with another jingle—the wind chime was bolted near the inside top of the door—then turned to climb the stairs. What the heck, I could at least find out what was up there.

The landing was dim. To my right was a closed door with a line of light shining under it. A small sign on the door read:

THE SECOND ANSWER

Faint music sounded. The door opened a crack, and a woman peeked out. She looked about twenty, though it was hard to guess her age when I only saw half her face and a lot of wavy blond hair. She gave me half a smile and closed the door.

To my left stood an open door, and beyond the threshold was a nest. Or maybe it was a spiderweb? The floor was covered by a spiky green-and-brown rug. It looked like something that could swallow you up.

Velvet ribbons in different dark colors lined the walls. Two shadowy glass-fronted display cases faced each other, with fat pale candles burning on top of them and lots of dim objects crowded inside them. Between them stood a low round table with more lit candles on it, plus an oversize deck of cards and a crystal ball. Beyond the table, a big chair was piled with little square and star-shaped pillows, and in the middle of the pillows sat a woman.

She was spider-leg skinny, lost in a dress that wrapped her up in shades of gray from her neck to her wrists and toes. Her hair rayed out around her head in shades of gray and silver, too. Her face looked young and old at the same time, soft but not wrinkled, like an overripe peach.

She didn't look anything like my mom's mom, Gran, my least favorite grandparent, who came into the house once a year around Thanksgiving and reorganized everything without asking, including my room. But there was something about the woman in the chair that reminded me of Gran. Maybe her dark eyes, which stared at me as though she were figuring out all the ways I was wrong.

"Knock knock," I said in a shaky voice. I glanced back at the stairs. I could still leave.

Maybe she could solve my problem.

"Take off your shoes and come in," said the woman. She had the butterscotch voice I'd heard from below, smooth and somehow soothing.

"I don't think you want me to do that," I said. "My feet stink."

"That's all right." She waved a thin hand toward the counter on the right. "I have incense." Two sticks burned there, sending up swirls of pale gray smoke.

I slipped off my canvas shoes. My feet did stink but, hey, she said it was okay. I left my shoes by the door and stepped across the threshold. She pointed to a spot just the other side of the table from her. "Come. Sit. Tell me what you need."

Okay, so I had to walk across the creepy carpet. In my socks. I stepped on it. It was like walking on woven sticks, or dried finger bones. It crackled under my feet, but it didn't eat me.

I made it to where she had pointed, slid off my backpack, sat on it, and looked at her.

She wrinkled her nose. My feet had more power than her incense! Then she made some signs with her fingers and waved her hand. My feet tingled.

The stink was gone.

The back of my neck buzzed like I had Spidey sense. Weird had just gotten weirder.

Okay. Maybe she was a witch.

Panic!

If she was a witch, though, maybe she really *could* fix things. I took some deep breaths to slow my heartbeat.

"How may I help you?" she asked.

"I don't know," I said. I wasn't sure I wanted witch help. Maybe that was the only thing that *could* help me, though. I had a thought. "Does this cost money? All I have is one fifty." I had planned to spend it on a Coke at the 7-Eleven on the walk home with Reed.

"There are other ways to pay," she said. She smiled. Some of her teeth were pointed, like a shark's.

"Like how?" I said. What if she charged an arm or a leg? And made me watch her eat it?

"Tell me your problem, and we'll discuss."

I thought about my problem.

I had lost my best and only friend, and I didn't know how to get him back.

Should I ask for Reed to be shorter again? No. He was enjoying his tallness. There was no guarantee he'd like me if he were short again.

"I need to be taller," I said.

"That will likely happen in time," she said. Now her smile looked like any grown-up's does when they tell you that. Really irritating.

"I need it to happen sooner." I squeezed my left hand in my right. Dad said it didn't help to ask the right questions if you were asking the wrong person. What if she was the right person, and this was the wrong question? My stomach churned.

She closed her eyes. A wrinkle appeared like a slot above her nose, and then she nodded. She slid off the big bowl of a chair, went to one of the glass cases, and opened a door on the back. "You'll need this." She pulled out a little crystal bottle with a yellow glass stopper.

"What is it?"

"It will make you taller." She set the bottle on the table in front of me.

"How?" The liquid inside the bottle was silvery green, and it glowed a little.

"One drop in a glass of milk three times a day will do it." She nodded.

"How long will it take?"

"I can't tell you for sure. Everyone reacts differently, some people much more quickly than others. It shouldn't take longer than a week."

I picked up the bottle, pulled out the stopper, and sniffed. The potion smelled like summer, mowed lawns, sunlight, barbecue. Summer, back before I knew Reed was going to leave me behind. Or maybe it was next summer, when we'd be together again, running through backyards, through sprinklers, pretending we were avoiding an alien invasion, planning our next adventure. Longing twisted in me. I wanted this.

I put the stopper in the bottle and set it on the table. How could I afford it?

The witch cocked her head, studying me, then gave me another smile. She went to the other glass case and pulled out a small, flat, purple pillow. She set that on the table in front of me, too. "In return, I would like three hours of uninterrupted sleep."

"What? How can I give you that?"

"You're young. You have lots of nice sleep in you. Put your head on the pillow and say, three times, 'I give up an hour of my best sleep.'"

Even though I wasn't sure I believed any of this, I was still worried. I checked the potion again, with its promise of summer and size. I studied the pillow. It was shiny and soft, and gave off an herb smell, like the dried leaves my mom crushed and sprinkled over chicken before putting it in the oven. I looked at the witch.

I didn't always sleep all that well. Nightmares were kind of a specialty of mine. Every once in a while, though, I did sleep okay.

"The choice is yours," she said as she settled back onto her chair.

Put my head down and say a stupid sentence. I could do that. I laid my head on the pillow and closed my eyes. Its smell made me hungry. "I give up an hour of my best sleep," I said. The pillow rustled under my ear. It felt like something drained out of my head.

Spooked, I lifted my head and stared at the witch. She raised her eyebrows, shrugged, and reached across the table for the potion bottle.

No. I needed it! I put my head on the pillow again. "I give up an hour of my best sleep." A rustle, and the sensation of an ocean stirring in my head, then some of it pouring out of my ear into the pillow. My eyes burned a little, and my stomach lurched.

Creepy! I lifted my head.

The witch leaned forward again, her hand outstretched toward my potion.

"Wait!" I was so close! I'd already paid for two-thirds of the potion. I could do the rest.

"I give up an hour of my best sleep," I said a third time. The room whirled. I had to close my eyes or I'd be sick. I groaned and lifted my head off the pillow, then sagged back onto the bristly rug, feeling like cooked pasta.

"Thank you, young man," said the witch.

I opened my eyes and saw her rise and take the pillow. She tucked it among the others on her chair. I wondered if they all had people's sleep in them, or if she collected other things. She left and came back with a plate, which she set on the table. "When you feel up to it, here's a cookie," she said. "It will make you feel better."

I lay there. When the room stopped spinning, I sat up. The cookie was shaped like a cat. All my mom's advice about not taking sweets from strangers went through my head, and then I thought, *I just gave this woman three hours of my best sleep so I can drink something she made. If I survive the cookie, maybe the potion won't be poisonous, either.*

I took a bite. It tasted great, as good as the smell of fresh bread when you walk by a bakery. I wolfed the rest of the cookie and felt a lot better.

I managed to get to my feet. "Okay, then," I said, and pulled my backpack on. I reached for the potion and tucked it into my pocket.

The witch smiled. "Good luck."

I put on my shoes and raced down the stairs and out into the chilly evening, slamming the jingling door behind me. I checked my watch. It was almost suppertime. I should have been home two hours ago. How long had I lain on the rug? Mom would boil me in oil.

Luckily, Mom thought I'd been out for a walk with Reed. She wasn't mad, even though I'd missed homework time. "I'm glad you guys got back together," she said. "I know you had a lonely summer."

"You should branch out," Dad said. "Reed's a great guy, but you need more friends."

I gnawed on a chicken leg so I wouldn't have to answer. Easy to talk about making more friends. Not so easy to find them if nobody liked you. Being taller would fix that, I figured—it sure worked for

Reed—but I didn't drink my first drop of the potion until bedtime. I didn't want to suddenly get taller in front of my parents.

I woke up in the middle of the night when I bumped my head against the wall. I reached for the bedside light and knocked it right off the table. My feet were sticking off the end of the bed. Something gripped me around my stomach. I sat up and heard cloth rip. The bed creaked under me. I flailed around until I found the lamp on the floor. I switched it on. Luckily, the lightbulb hadn't broken.

I could see why I'd knocked the lamp over. I wasn't just taller. I was *bigger in every direction.* The waistband of my pajama bottoms had stretched as far as it could. I edged a thumb under the band, and it broke. I'd already ripped out of my top.

I wrapped the bedspread around me and stood. My head brushed the ceiling! I took a step and the room shuddered. My second step was softer. I had to duck to get through the doorway. I tiptoed down the hall to the bathroom. I ducked in, shut the door, and switched on the light.

With my eyes near the ceiling, I looked down on a lot of things I'd never seen the tops of before. Mostly what I noticed was dust, layers of it, in all the places nobody ever looked. Everything was so different.

I had to bend down to see myself in the bathroom mirror. I looked stretched out and strange. I totally didn't make sense. I didn't look like a grown-up; I looked like a giant boy. A freak. No way was this going to win me any friends, especially not Reed.

"Knock knock," I muttered.

"Who's there?" asked the giant boy in the mirror.

"Despair," I said. I left off the punch line about the spare tire being flat.

None of my clothes would fit me. Not even Dad's clothes would. I couldn't go to school like this! My parents might take me to the hospital to find out what had happened. I didn't think doctors would know how to deal with witchcraft. Nobody did. Except the witch.

The witch! I didn't know her name or phone number. I would have to go to her place and get her to change me back! Right now, before dawn, while most people were asleep.

I stopped in the hallway at Dad's tool drawer, fished out bungee cords and twine, and went to check my closet and dresser. I was right. Nothing I owned fit me now. I had no shoes big enough for my feet, so I wrapped towels around them, tied them on with twine, then bungeed blankets around me the best I could. I wore the darkest one like a cape.

The walk down Burns Street was creepy. Everything was dark and quiet, which I liked, but I was still scared. Every time a car drove by, I squashed into a doorway. My one happy thought was that no one would try to hurt me—I was bigger than anybody I'd ever met.

Luckily, I made it to the witch's place without running into anyone. Of course the door was locked. I looked for a doorbell, but there wasn't one. Even the sign had disappeared from over the door.

I knocked. Nothing happened. I knocked longer and louder. Finally, a light switched on at the top of the stairs, and someone peered down at me. It was pretty dim in the stairwell, but I could see that it wasn't the witch. It was the woman with wavy blond hair who had peeked out the other door at the top of the stairs. She was carrying a baseball bat. She came down the stairs. "What do you want?" she yelled through the door. She looked at me closely. "Oh, it's you."

"Where is she?" I asked. "Where's the witch?"

"Gone."

"What?"

"She's my grandma. She has lots of grandkids. She only stops in once a year for a few days. She solves some people's problems, teaches me a few tricks of the trade, and then she's gone again."

"Where'd she go?" I asked.

"To the next grandkid's, probably. Maybe my cousin Zack—he lives in Canada."

Canada! It might as well be the other side of the world. Everything inside me sagged. I folded slowly to the sidewalk and wrapped my arms around my knees. I started to cry. I couldn't help it.

The door opened. "Hey," she said. "Hey."

I wiped my eyes and peered up at her.

"How old are you?" she asked.

"Twelve."

"She turned you into a giant? Why'd she do that?"

"I just wanted to be taller."

"Why?"

No way was I going to tell her the real reason. I turned away from her and stared up the street. I could walk around and grab streetlights, if I felt like it, reach into second-story windows. Maybe I could join a freak show and people would pay to look at me. But that would be wrong. I was the observer. I didn't want anybody looking at me.

"How'd she do it?" asked the woman.

"She gave me a potion."

"How much did you take?"

"Just a drop. She said I should take a drop in milk three times a day, and I'd get taller."

"Wow. It shouldn't have worked that fast or that well. You must have atypical magic chemistry!"

"Great." I looked at my giant hands and feet and wondered if I could give the potion to my clothes to make them fit me.

"But listen," she went on. "If you've taken only one dose, it should wear off soon. It's not permanent until you've taken it five times."

"Really? Really?" I climbed to my feet. She came up to my waist.

"Yeah. Go home. You'll be all right."

"Thank you," I said. I wanted to hug her, but she was still holding the baseball bat, and I wasn't sure of my own strength. "Thanks."

"My name's Larissa. Bring that potion to me, and I'll trade you something for it. I have a feeling it might be good for my vegetables."

"Thank you," I said again. I couldn't seem to stop saying it. I turned and ran all the way home, even though I lost my feet towels along the way. By the time I got to my front door, I had shrunk enough that I didn't need to duck to enter.

I fell into bed but couldn't get back to sleep. I imagined the witch somewhere with her head on the purple pillow, cashing in on my sleep. I reread some of my favorite manga, glancing up every once in a while to see how much farther away the end of the bed was from my toes.

When morning finally came, I took the shower of all showers. I was singing because I was my right size again! My clothes fit!

Dad told me to cut down on the morning cheer. He had a headache because a loud noise had woken him up and he hadn't been able to get back to sleep.

"What was it?" Mom asked.

"I have no idea," said Dad. "I came downstairs to see what it was, but I didn't find any sign of a break-in." He went into the living room. "Now, will you look at that? Giant footprints on the carpet!"

"What?" said Mom. She went to look at the footprints, then came back, her face pale. "We'd better change the locks."

"Knock knock," I said.

My parents groaned. They always did when I said that. "Who's there?" Dad asked.

"Me."

"Me who?" Dad said.

"Me," I said again. "I made those footprints. Kind of a joke. Sorry. It was just me."

It was one of those good news/bad news situations. I was myself again, but I still had my Reed problem—no one to walk home with.

I stopped on Burns Street after school to give the potion to Larissa. She gave me a green heart-shaped stone.

"What's this for?" I asked.

"Just keep it in your pocket," she said.

The next day, I had the heart in my pocket as I headed home from school. Derek, this cool guy who's always inventing crazy stuff out of straws and Popsicle sticks and paper clips, and actually laughs at my knock-knocks, said, "Hey, Mike."

"Hey," I said. I didn't even know he knew my name.

"You going down Burns Street?"

"Yeah."

"Me, too."

EYES ON IMOGENE

by Richard Peck

It was the afternoon of February fourteenth, and my sister Imogene was soaking her mail.

Back in those days, you sent your Valentines from the post office, stamped. Girls counted how many they got. Imogene did. They also thought somebody might write a secret message of love under the stamp.

So they had to go to work and soak all the stamps off to see. Imogene did. When I drifted into the kitchen, she snatched up all the soaked envelopes and ripped them into confetti.

I took it there was nothing written under those stamps. She stood tapping a foot at the sink, waiting for me to go away. But I was her little brother. It was my job to pester her, and I didn't like to shirk it.

"No message of secret passion yet?" I inquired of the big red bow on the back of her head. But there was still a small pile of envelopes unopened on the drainboard.

"Go ahead on," I said. "Peel off them other stamps. Don't mind me."

"After you're gone," she said to the kitchen wall.

But her hand was twitching toward the last envelopes. It beat me how many Valentines she got. I used to think she sent them to herself. But I wasn't sure now. She was at the high school, and anything can happen there. She was being too ladylike today to chase me outside and off the porch. Besides, she looked down and saw an envelope unlike the rest, asking to be opened.

The envelope wasn't a Valentine color, and it was limp and stained, like it had been soaked already. You could barely read Imogene's name and our address on it. The stamp was already gone, the postmark blurred. There was something kind of nasty about it. I personally thought it smelled funny. Something smelled funny. Imogene wanted to wipe her hands on her apron, but curiosity got the better of her.

She tore at the envelope. Inside, a flimsy page unfolded, reading:

ROSES ARE RED
VIOLETS ARE BLUE
I'M OUTSIDE THE WINDOW
LOOKING AT YOU

I read that around her arm, and it gave me the creeps. She couldn't help but glance at the window. We both did. There was nothing but evening out there, and the porch.

Then at the bottom of the flimsy page, a name, very clear:

Earl

Earl? I thought, and something slithered down my spine. Imogene turned on me. The paper shook in her hand. The only Earl we knew of was Earl Youngblood. He'd dropped out of the high school better than a year ago, to join the navy.

"Did you send this?" Imogene brandished the limp sheet in my face. "Because it isn't funny, and I'll find out."

Earl Youngblood had sunk on the battleship *Maine* when it blew up in the harbor at Havana, last year around Valentine's Day. True, they never found his complete body. For the funeral they buried an empty sailor suit and a finger bone with his class ring on it.

"Not funny in the slightest." Imogene's voice wobbled all over the kitchen. But she could tell by looking, I hadn't sent the thing. Imogene could always see right through me.

I suspected Whip Chandler, who was more or less my best friend. Though he was only in eighth grade, I happened to know he had eyes for Imogene. I'd happened to see the hair ribbon he'd stolen from her, tied on his watch fob. But what high-school girl would look at a Valentine from an eighth grader? Though I think Whip had repeated a grade sometime earlier.

I caught up with him after school that next day. "Whip," I inquired, "you send a verse or anything to Imogene for Valentine's?"

"What good would that do me?" He was a big, overgrown kid. He looked like a man to me.

"You sure?"

He made a fist, so I guessed he was sure. I told him about the message signed "Earl."

"Earl Youngblood?" We were trudging along, but Whip slowed. "He's at the bottom of the harbor down in wherever, isn't he? That place where the war started."

Either that, or sending Valentine verses from the post office. I still suspected Whip of trying to get Imogene's attention any way he could.

Snow was falling on ice. A horse was down, over at the cross street, so Whip and I had to help with that. When we were on our way again, I said, "Was Earl Youngblood sweet on Imogene?"

Whip looked down on me. "Everybody's sweet on Imogene. You just can't see it because she's your sister."

Oh.

"And you're just a kid." Whip shrugged me off, kind of disgusted, and we split up and headed home.

Then there was a big ruckus that same night. Mother and Dad were in the front room after supper, their feet to the stove. Imogene was up in her room. I was somewhere, hiding from chores. We had us a hired girl who cooked and washed up. Her name was Agnes, and she was real thin and nervous.

When she let out that scream, you could hear it downtown. People did. There followed the sound of breaking crockery. We all pounded into the kitchen to see Agnes bent double and blubbering.

"Well, it was not the best set," Mother said, meaning the broken dishes. "Agnes, take the apron down from your face."

She was white as flour and pointing to the window. "It was horrible," she blurted, "a ghastly figure in clouds of smoke. He pointed to his heart."

Agnes pointed to hers.

"His eyes burned like hot coals," she moaned. "When he seen me, he vanished."

You'd think nobody'd ever looked at Agnes before, which nobody had.

"How tall, Agnes?" I inquired, and she put her jittering hand up about Whip's height.

I was sure it was Whip. In fact, I thought I'd given him the idea. The so-called smoke was from his steamy breath. It was zero that night. Agnes had added the burning-coal eyes.

Dad had to put on his overshoes and bundle up to take Agnes home. She said if this kind of thing kept up, she'd quit.

The next day, I caught up with Whip. "Were you out last night?" I inquired.

"No," he said. "Where?"

"On our back porch, looking in, pointing to your heart?"

"I spent all evening at my workbench," he said, "shaving shingles."

"You got any witnesses?" I said.

He made a fist, so that was good enough for me.

"Well, if it wasn't you and it wasn't me, who was it?"

"Who was who?" Whip said.

"The ghastly figure on our back porch who vanished when he saw it was Agnes, not Imogene."

"Could have been anybody from the high school. Everybody's sweet on—"

"But who?" I said.

So we decided to stake out the back porch and nab whoever it was. Whip played along in hopes of a glimpse of Imogene. I wanted to get to the bottom of this. If Agnes kept throwing crockery, we'd run out of it. Besides, the whole thing had me worried.

I slipped out after supper and met Whip behind the barn. A pale moon played through bare branches. It was so cold, the world squeaked, and I thought I'd lose my ears. There was no place to hide where you could see the back porch. We were dancing to keep from freezing when we just gave up and went our separate ways home.

When I nagged Whip to stand guard the night after that, he made a fist, and I took that for a no.

Anyway, no ghastly figure or anybody from the high school peered into our kitchen on the nights that followed. When I asked Imogene what she'd done with the mysterious verse in the limp envelope, she said she'd stuck it in the stove.

It was a hard winter. Winters were, back then, not like now. There wasn't a thaw till almost April, when Mother had us doing spring cleaning. My job was to clean off the back porch and see if it needed a coat of paint. Having no choice, I set to work one Saturday morning.

Then, right there on the floor under the kitchen window where I was sweeping, I spied a long curl of something frozen in the last of the ice. It looked like slimy seaweed. I looked closer. Scattered all about were seashells. Seashells, crusted with hard little grains of sparkling sand.

I thought hard about it, squatting there on the porch. Where had Whip Chandler come by something like seaweed and sandy seashells all these hundreds of miles from an ocean? In the dead of winter? Whip Chandler had never been out of town.

When I couldn't figure out how he'd pulled that, I swept the seaweed and those shells loose from the ice and over the side of the porch.

And I did my level best never to think about them again.

THE THREE-EYED MAN

by R.L. Stine

When the three-eyed man moved into the house on the corner, we kids tried to ignore him.

I had to pass his house to go to school. But I always rode my bike on the other side of the street. I pedaled hard and stared into his front window—and hoped I didn't find him staring back at me.

My dog, Rusty, is a Lab-shepherd mix. He's big, but he's the friendliest dog in the world. Rusty started to bark whenever I walked him near the three-eyed man's house.

Once when I was walking Rusty, the man came out on the front stoop to get his mail. And I got a real good look at the third eye. It was perched at the bridge of his nose, tucked in right where his eyebrows met.

Rusty bared his teeth and started barking ferociously, the way he does when he spots a squirrel. He tugged so hard, I almost lost my grip on his leash.

"Rusty—NO!" I shouted, pulling him back with all my strength. "No! Let's go home!"

The three-eyed man looked up from his mail and gave us a wave.

I gasped. And a chill rolled down my back.

He wasn't trying to be *friendly*—was he?

I tugged Rusty home. I found Dad in his workshop, leaning over his glue gun. Dad's hobby is making sculptures out of little pieces of wood.

Dad was wearing his denim work overalls over a blue T-shirt. He is very tall and lanky. And he's nearsighted. So he has to bend way down to get close to his sculpture.

I told Dad about seeing the three-eyed man and how Rusty wanted to attack him.

"Rusty was acting on instinct, David," Dad said. He didn't look up from his glue gun. "He knows the man is different."

I watched Dad work. He had a stack of little round pieces of wood. They looked like coins. He was using them to make some kind of bird.

"The man on the corner has the Third Sight," Dad said. "He has powers that we don't have. He can see things our eyes can't see. I think you should stay away from him."

I didn't need to be told. I was already staying away. But I couldn't stop thinking about that third eye on the bridge of his nose.

I wanted to ask Dad what the Third Sight is. But he doesn't like to talk while he works. So I hurried upstairs to lunch.

Two days later, the three-eyed man came after me.

* * *

It was a sunny morning. Already very hot. The lawns sparkled under the bright sun.

My bike had a flat tire, so I had to walk to school.

"Hey, David! David—wait up!"

My friend Aaron came running out of his house. He crossed the street, running, lowered his shoulder, and bumped me so hard I staggered backward.

Aaron is a short, chubby, goofy kinda guy who likes to bump people and wrestle and tackle them for no reason. He just thinks it's funny.

So we were bumping and trying to trip each other as we walked. Aaron laughed as my backpack fell off my shoulders. And when I bent over to pick it up, he head-butted me in the back and I stumbled face-first to the ground.

"Ha-ha! Eat dirt!" Aaron cried. It's his favorite expression.

I grabbed him and pulled him down, and we started to wrestle. With a powerful heave, I spun him onto his back and pinned his shoulders in the dirt.

"Look out—we're in someone's flowers!" Aaron cried.

I let out a gasp and let go of Aaron. Breathing hard, I gazed at the crushed tulips around us. And then I turned my eyes to the house at the top of the lawn.

"Oh, noooo," I moaned.

The three-eyed man's house. We had ruined his flowers.

Was he watching? Bright sunlight glared off his front window. I couldn't see inside.

"Aaron—let's go!" I cried. I pulled him to his feet. He had a yellow tulip stuck to his shirt. I plucked it off and tossed it to the ground. "Hurry!"

I started to walk fast. Aaron fixed his backpack. Then he trotted to catch up to me.

I heard a door slam. But I didn't turn around. I just kept walking fast.

We were crossing Bridge Street when I heard soft thuds on the sidewalk behind us.

I turned and saw the three-eyed man coming after us.

His hands were balled into fists, and he swung his arms as he walked.

He was big—tall and wide and powerful-looking. He was dressed all in black. He had a baggy black sweatshirt pulled down over black sweatpants. His big belly bounced with each lumbering stride.

His face was bright red. He had straw-colored hair sticking out in all directions.

All three eyes were narrowed at us in a cold stare. Two eyes were brown. The middle eye was yellow. His mouth was twisted in a tight scowl.

"What's he gonna do?" Aaron cried. "We only wrecked a few flowers."

"I—I don't know," I stammered. "Let's *move!*" I gave Aaron a push, and we both began to jog.

Behind us, I could hear the man's footsteps thud faster on the sidewalk. He was jogging, too.

My dad's words repeated in my mind: *"He has the Third Sight. Stay away from him."*

Only two blocks to school. If we could make it there, we'd be safe.

I began to jog faster, leaving Aaron behind. Sweat ran down my forehead. My legs felt shaky and weak.

I glanced back. The three-eyed man was gaining on us. Swinging his fists hard. I could feel his eyes burning into my back.

The Third Sight . . .

I grabbed Aaron by the arm. "We . . . we can't outrun him," I gasped.

Panting hard, I spun around to face the man. Aaron uttered a weak cry.

My legs almost buckled.

The three-eyed man strode up to me. He raised a big fist.

"I'm sorry!" The words burst out of me in a high, shrill voice. "Sorry about your flowers."

He grumbled something under his breath. Then he stuck out a big hand and gave me something. "You dropped this," he said. He had a low, whispery voice.

I grabbed it in my trembling hand. My wallet. It must have fallen from my backpack. "Uh . . . thank you," I stammered.

He closed his middle eye and stared hard at me. "I can see that you will need me soon," he said.

"Huh?" I gasped. "What do you mean?"

He opened the middle eye. It gazed at me, wet and yellow as an egg yolk. "You can repay me then," he muttered.

The words sent an icy shiver to the back of my neck.

He didn't explain. He nodded his big head, turned, and began to lumber back to his house.

I tucked the wallet into my jeans pocket. My hand was shaking like crazy. And my heart was pounding so hard, I could *hear* it!

"Wow. Scary guy!" Aaron exclaimed. "Did he say you would see him again?"

"See him again? No way," I said, shaking my head. "No way."

But of course I was wrong.

A few nights later, Mom asked me to take Rusty for a long walk. "The poor guy hasn't had any exercise in days," she said.

So I took Rusty to the Stimson Woods, a big forest area a few blocks from school. It was a warm, clear night. A pale full moon hung low overhead. The wind smelled all piney and fresh.

Rusty loves to smell all the smells and run over the dead leaves and through the thick trees. He gets so excited, he whimpers.

As we walked deeper into the woods, the moonlight disappeared. The shadows deepened to black. The air grew cooler.

"Rusty, let's turn back," I said.

I heard a flapping sound overhead. Bats? As I gazed up, I felt a hard tug on the leash. Then I heard the sharp crackle of leaves— Rusty running fast.

"Hey!" I let out a startled cry. The big dog had slipped out of his collar. I couldn't see him in the darkness. But I heard him running, running free.

"Rusty—come back!" I shouted. I hurtled after him. Stumbled over a tree limb or something. And fell hard to the dirt.

"Rusty—stay! Stay!" I cried. "Rusty—!"

I pulled myself to my feet. And listened.

Silence now. Birds cooing in a high branch nearby. Wind whispering through the fresh spring leaves.

"Rusty? Hey—Rusty!" My voice cracked.

I had a heavy feeling of panic. *Oh, please*, I thought, *don't run away, Rusty. Don't get lost in the woods.*

I cupped my hands around my mouth and shouted. "Rusty! Rusty, come! Rusty!"

In my panic, I started to run after him in one direction. Spun around wildly. Tore off in another direction. Shouting the dog's name over and over.

He'd never done this before. He'd never slipped his leash. He'd never run off on his own.

"Rusty? Rusty?"

Silence all around. The birds cooed again. A big tree branch cracked and rattled in the wind.

I had no choice. I couldn't just stand there in the middle of the dark woods. "Rusty—I'm going home!" I shouted. "Home! Are you going to follow me? Rusty—come!"

I trudged home with my hands buried deep in my jeans pockets. I kicked leaves and tromped loudly on the ground, hoping Rusty would hear me.

But no sign of the dog.

And when I burst into the den and told Dad what had happened, I couldn't keep the tears from my eyes. I was really upset and scared.

"Don't worry, David," Dad said, putting a hand on my shoulder. "Rusty will find his way home. He's a smart dog. He won't get lost. You'll see. He'll be back tonight. Or maybe tomorrow morning."

"Dad, what if he can't find his way?" I asked in a trembling voice. "He'll DIE out there!"

"He'll be here when you wake up tomorrow," Dad said. "I'll bet you."

Dad lost that bet. The next morning, I jumped out of bed and eagerly ran downstairs. No Rusty.

I opened the front door and gazed up and down the street. No Rusty. He wasn't in the backyard, either.

I couldn't eat my breakfast. I felt as if I had a heavy rock in my stomach.

Mom took the car and went driving around the neighborhood, searching for Rusty. Dad and I walked to the woods. I tried to retrace my steps. We shouted Rusty's name over and over.

The dog didn't come.

I wanted to keep searching for Rusty. But Dad said I had to go to school.

I sat in class like a statue. I don't think I heard a word anyone said. All day, I just kept thinking about my poor, lost dog.

When the last bell rang, I ran all the way home. I searched for Rusty in every yard. I burst into the house, shouting his name.

No one was home. And no dog.

I tossed my backpack against the wall. I gripped the back of the couch with both hands, shut my eyes, and tried to force my heart to stop racing.

I knew what I had to do.

Just thinking about it sent chill after chill down my body. But I knew I had no choice.

I had to go see the three-eyed man.

The tulips in his front yard were still bent and broken. I shuddered as I walked past them, up the driveway to his front door.

I kept gritting my teeth. My muscles felt all tight.

I knew it was fear.

The three-eyed man had predicted I'd need him soon. And here I was.

He had the Third Sight. Maybe that meant he could tell me where to find my dog.

I didn't see a doorbell. I raised my hand to knock on the front door—and it swung open. He stood there with a tight grin on his face, as if he'd been expecting me.

His middle eye was closed. His brown eyes flashed, and his grin widened. He was wearing the same outfit—black sweatshirt and black sweatpants.

"Enter," he rumbled. He stepped back to make room.

I took a deep breath and walked inside. I gazed around the living room. The walls were red brick. They were covered with strange paintings. The paintings all looked like big smears of color. The couches and chairs were all black leather. I saw a line of furry toy animals on the mantel.

"My dog—" I choked out.

"I can find him for you," the three-eyed man said softly.

I gasped. "How did you know he is lost?" I blurted out.

He opened the yellow eye. "I have the Third Sight," he said.

I heard a clock ticking loudly in the next room. The loud, fast ticks matched my heartbeats. My mouth suddenly felt too dry to talk.

"I will tell you where to find your dog," the man said. "But then you must return. And pay the price."

I swallowed. "I don't have much money," I said.

"I won't ask you for money," he replied softly. Then he leaned forward. The yellow eye floated right above me.

"You love your dog, don't you," the man said. "You'd give almost anything to have him back, wouldn't you?"

"Uh . . . almost," I stammered.

He shut his three eyes and concentrated for a long time. Finally, he said, "I see him."

My heart skipped a beat. "Where?" I cried. "Is he okay?"

It took him a long time to answer. Then he opened his eyes and narrowed them at me. "Do you know the pond in Stimson Woods that used to have fish?"

I nodded. "Yes. Rusty and I walk there sometimes."

"There is a deep ravine behind the pond," the man said. "It's filled with broken tree limbs. Look in the ravine."

"Is . . . is Rusty okay?" I asked again.

"Look in the ravine," he repeated.

He rubbed the yellow eye with one finger. "Afterward, I'll see you back here, David."

I didn't know what to say. Was Rusty okay? Was he really in the ravine behind the pond?

The three-eyed man pushed open the front door, and I stepped outside. The sky had turned dark, with black storm clouds rolling low overhead.

I ran to Stimson Woods. I was crazy . . . out of my mind . . . frantic. I didn't stop running or look when I crossed Peach Street. A car squealed to a stop. I heard a woman screaming at me. But I didn't look back.

I felt a few cold raindrops slap my forehead as I darted into the trees. The wind rattled the dead leaves all around me. Tree limbs shivered.

I felt as if the woods had come ALIVE!

I ran too fast. I slammed my head against a low limb. I kept tripping over roots and fallen twigs.

The small pond glowed black under the dark, stormy sky. I slipped in the wet mud on its banks and kept running.

To the ravine.

Rain pattered the ground. A blast of cold wind pushed me back.

The ravine was a deep hole. Like a canyon that had been cut into the ground. I gazed down at fallen trees, broken limbs, thick, dead shrubs, and underbrush.

Lightning flashed. And then a sharp crack of thunder seemed to shake the ground.

The steady rain blurred my vision. I saw a white sneaker down there. A red square of cloth flapping in the wind. Some soda cans.

"Rusty!" I screamed over another boom of thunder. "Rusty— are you here?"

And then I saw him.

He was struggling . . . pulling . . . whining. . . . His back legs trapped in the thick brambles.

"Rusty!"

My heart pounding, I slid down the side of the ravine. The dog saw me but kept whining and struggling to free himself from the prickly brush.

"I'm here, boy. Don't worry."

I pulled a burr off his left ear. His fur was thick with sticks and caterpillars and dead leaves. His eyes were wild. His snout was all frothy. His tongue hung over the side of his mouth, and he uttered horrible groans as he struggled.

71

"Easy, boy. I'm here. Easy, Rusty."

I grabbed the brambles and pulled them apart. Thorns dug into my hands. But I ignored the pain. I pulled the brambles until Rusty was free.

I rubbed my cut hands on my jeans. I shook off rainwater. "Let's go home, boy! Come on. Let's go!"

He jumped on me once. I guess that was his way of saying thanks.

Then he began loping toward home, his tail wagging, head bobbing up and down as if nothing had happened.

By the time I got him home, I was drenched to the skin. But the rain felt good. Clean and refreshing.

Still no one home. I fed Rusty and gave him a big biscuit as a treat.

Was I happy? Yes. I was thrilled to have good old Rusty home safe and sound.

But I knew I didn't have long to enjoy it. I had one more thing to do.

I had to go pay the three-eyed man for finding my dog.

The rain had stopped, but the sky was still dark as night. A river of water ran down the side of the street. I jumped over deep puddles as I made my way slowly to the house on the corner.

I stopped in front of the house and gazed at it. The windows were completely dark.

I tried to convince myself that the three-eyed man meant me no harm.

He found Rusty for me.

He used his special sight to help me.

He isn't going to ask for any big kind of payback.

So why did I have this sick feeling in my stomach?

I trudged up the driveway, onto his front stoop. Again, the door swung open before I knocked.

The three-eyed man waved me inside without a word. I followed him into the living room. The only light came from two flickering candles on the coffee table. It sent long shadows dancing over the brick walls.

"You—you were right," I stammered. "I found Rusty—right where you said."

"I know," the man said in his low, whispery voice. "And now you've come to pay me."

I nodded. I tried to say yes but my voice cracked.

"It won't hurt," the man said.

I blinked. "Hurt? What do you mean?"

"Your payment, David." He stared at me intently with all three eyes.

I took a step back. "What is it?" I managed to choke out. "What do you want?"

"Follow me," he said. He moved to the back of the living room and pushed open a door. "Into the den."

I forced my trembling legs to cooperate. I stepped into the den.

He flashed on the ceiling light—and I SCREAMED.

The wall in front of me—it was covered with EYES!

Eyeballs from the ceiling to the floor. Row after row of them, staring straight out from the wall.

I couldn't move. I couldn't breathe. I stared back at them.

73

Brown eyes . . . blue . . . silvery eyes . . . green . . .

"Yes, they're real," the man said. "But they're of no use to me anymore."

"I . . . I don't understand," I whispered.

"After I use the Third Sight, my middle eye loses its power," he said. "I can only use the middle eye once. Then I need to replace it with a fresh one."

I took a step back. "No—please. . . ."

"It won't hurt," he said. "I used the Third Sight for you. Now I need one of your eyes. It's a fair payment, David. You know I'm being fair."

A shuddering cry escaped my throat. "No! I *can't*! NO!"

I tried to run, but my whole body was frozen in terror.

He moved quickly. He wrapped his hands around my head. Then he *plucked* out one of my eyes.

"AAAAAAIIIIIIII!"

I screamed—and waited for the pain.

But he had told the truth. It didn't hurt.

"My eye!" I cried. "I don't believe it! My eye!"

My hand went up to the empty socket. It was wet. I could feel soft, mushy skin in there.

"Now I have only *three eyes*!" I cried. "Only three! Now I'm just like *you*!"

He smiled. "That's not true," he said. "You still have the eight eyeballs on your fingertips."

I raised my hands and stared at my eight finger eyes.

The eyes trembled on the edges of my fingers. My whole body trembled.

Okay, okay, I told myself. *It didn't hurt. And I can still see clearly. But what will my five moms and dads say when I come home with only eleven eyes?*

BONES

by Margaret Mahy

There was something strange about the house they were moving into. Pete knew this immediately. It was as if something was recognizing him, even though he had never been there before. Something came to meet him and began pulling him inside. Pete leaned backward a little. His mother must have noticed his hesitation. She was good at noticing things. She had had a lot of practice.

"We won't be here long," she said in a comforting voice. "It's just a stopover place until our own house is finished. And when that happens, we'll have our own space again . . . our own furniture, our own toys and pictures and things."

"I think it's just great," said Pete's sister, Gwen. "I wouldn't mind living here forever. It's so—so *rich*."

This furnished house they were renting until their own house was finished was certainly grand. There were velvet cushions on the chairs. The ceilings were not just flat but curved above them in a majestic, echoing way. But the dark, shining rafters (curving, too) looked to Pete like giant ribs of brown bone, so he felt for a moment that this house was *swallowing* him. And then he felt as if he had somehow sent the idea of "bones" out into the air around him, and the house had tasted his idea, then welcomed it. This house was a house that knew exactly what bones were.

Over the fireplace in the sitting room hung a picture in a dusty frame. A large girl (who was probably about Pete's age) stared down at them, looking as if, just for a moment, the world was taking her by surprise.

"Does *she* live here?" Pete asked. "When we're *not* here, I mean."

"She used to, I think," said his mother. "But it was a long, long time ago. Look at the way she's dressed."

The girl was wearing a bulkier dress than any of the girls at Pete's school ever wore. On top of the dress, she was wearing a long, lumpy blue coat, and her feet were buttoned into black-and-white boots that looked as if they would be too heavy to walk in. Certainly no dancing in shoes like those. Pete couldn't help thinking it would be hard to play hide-and-seek (or any game at all) dressed as the girl in the picture was dressed. Her clothes had closed in on her. She was their prisoner.

The bedrooms were all in the second story of the house. The room that would be his for a few weeks had a big tree close to the window, scraping at the glass, as if it were ordering him to let it in. Pete felt strange, climbing upstairs to bed that night, leaving the kitchen world behind him, and all because, for some reason, he found this strange house scary. He imagined himself staying awake, on guard until morning, but, as it turned out, his bed was soft and comfortable and, after all, he was tired. Sighing and blinking, he fell asleep, no trouble at all. Asleep. But then, all of a sudden, he found he was wide-awake again, staring into darkness, knowing for sure that someone else was sharing that bedroom darkness with him. He took a deep breath and, as he did this, a thin voice came out of the night around him. It seemed to come from several directions at once.

"Dancing in the dark . . ." someone was singing. Not only that, something was rattling in time to the song . . . rattling just a little, but rattling clearly. Pete blinked—blinked again—sat up and peered into the shadows around him. The air in his bedroom was perfectly still— still with a curious, rigid stillness that made him feel that he, along with his bed, was somehow set in glass. No going forward! No going back! Even time was frozen. If there had been a clock in the room, it might have ticked, but it would never have moved on to tocking. And yet there was that rattling . . . that strange rattling . . . soft yet sharp as well. What could it be? There was certainly no breeze to rattle any door, to rattle coat hangers in a wardrobe—nothing to make a possibly loose window tremble a little.

"Dancing in the dark . . ." sang that voice again . . . that thin voice—a silver thread in the night—and though the sound was close to him in the bedroom, it also seemed to be coming to him across a great distance.

"Who's there?" Pete shouted. His own voice sounded all shuddery.

Well, that's okay, he thought. *I'm allowed to be frightened by midnight singing in a strange bedroom.* There was relief in shouting, even in shaky shouting. "Who's there?" he yelled again.

The singer stopped singing. The rattling stopped. But now there was a thudding in the hall outside his bedroom, and then his door swung sharply open. Someone turned on the light.

"Pete! Are you all right?" It was his mother. And, close behind her, peering nosily around her was his big sister, Gwen.

"He's probably got all scared, what with being in a strange house," said Gwen, sounding as if she were a grown-up talking about a mere toddler.

"I heard a funny sort of singing. Were you singing?" Pete asked, though he knew very well that the thin voice had not been a family one.

"No one was singing," said Pete's mother. "You must have been dreaming."

Pete was certain he had not been dreaming. His new bedroom was completely empty, yet only a moment ago someone had been sharing the room's darkness with him, singing and rattling in the night. He looked around, trying to work out just where that song and that faint, rhythmic rattling could possibly have come from. Nothing hanging from the door handle. Nothing rolling around the floor.

"You must have been dreaming," Gwen went on, as if she knew everything. "Little kids can get scared in a house they're not used to."

"I'm not little," said Pete indignantly. "And I'm not scared," he added, though, only a moment ago, he had certainly been terrified.

"You could sleep with Mom and Dad for the first nights," Gwen suggested, using that big-sister-comforting-a-baby voice. Pete hated it when she used that voice on him.

"Okay! Just dreaming!" he said quickly, though he was sure he had been wide-awake all the time, and listening with everyday ears, not dream ones.

"Well, call out again if you do have nightmares," his mother told him. "A new house can be a bit spooky to begin with." She gave him a hug. "I'll leave the door open a little bit and turn on the light in the hall."

The light was comforting, but Pete took a long time to go to sleep again. He lay there, remembering his fear and staring suspiciously toward his half-open door, thinking he might hear that thin song or that slight, rhythmic rattling once more. He could not work out just why that rattling had seemed so terrifying. After all, it was a rattling world. But at last, tired out from puzzling about it all, he fell asleep again and did not wake up until morning.

All family days were busy days, but the next day was particularly demanding. There was unpacking to do. Some things they needed to use while staying in this house, even though it was so completely furnished. Other boxes had to be repacked and stored in a spare room. Moving backward and forward, Pete looked up at those rib-rafters and imagined for a moment or two that he and his family were renting space in the belly of a monster merely *disguised* as a house. All the same, they worked together, they laughed together, they broke for lunch, worked again, and then had dinner, after which they settled down to watch television. It seemed odd to be watching familiar programs and commercials inside a man-eating house, but there was something comforting about familiar TV figures floating and flickering in the room with them.

"Heigh-ho! Bedtime for boys," said Pete's father at last. "Think you'll get by without any bad dreams tonight?"

"I don't know," Pete said, and saw Gwen grinning at him. "I'm not scared," he added defiantly.

"Well, it's a fine night tonight," said his mother. "Before you put on your pajamas, come out on the veranda and watch the moon rising. It's nearly full."

"Ghosts love a full moon," said Gwen, looking slyly at Pete.

"That's enough of that, Gwennie," said Pete's father, just a little crossly. "You'll make *me* nervous next, and then I'll be the one to have bad dreams."

"I'm not scared," Pete insisted yet again. "If a ghost did come into the room, I'd just talk to it. I'd say, 'Hello! Nice to meet you!'" As he said this, it suddenly seemed to him that being kind and polite might be a good way of coping with a ghost.

As it happened, he went to sleep quickly, tired out by all the sorting and shifting. But then, sometime much later, he woke up again, just as he had the night before. He did not open his eyes immediately but, under his eyelids, his eyes felt wide-awake. And his ears were wide-awake, too, hearing, once again, that strange rhythmic rattling and that thin voice singing its song.

"Dancing in the dark!" it sang. *"Free to dance! Free to dance!"*

The warm bed grew suddenly chilly around Pete. The sheets seemed to be spun out of ice. He tried to lie as still as possible . . . tried to make himself believe he was dreaming . . . tried to pretend he was still warm. But in the end he opened his eyes, sat up, and stared into that midnight bedroom. Well, he just had to.

The curtains were not quite drawn. Moonlight struggled through the gap and the glass behind it, lighting up part of the room. And—there was no doubt about it—something was dancing backward and forward across that band of moonlight, something that rattled in time to its own dancing.

Bones!

Bones spinning in the narrow shaft of silver, bones bowing to their own reflection in a mirror set in the wardrobe door, bones that rattled and clicked as they danced. Moonlight picked out grinning teeth, seeming to shift them a little, parting them to let that thin silver voice out into the room. Pete was looking at a dancing skeleton.

He stared at it, horrified. He tried to tell himself he really must be dreaming, but he knew he wasn't. There really were bones in his bedroom, spinning and rattling, singing and dancing. His mouth dropped open. He screamed out in fear.

Immediately the skeleton stood still. It stared back at him out of eye sockets, empty of eyes but flooded with a blackness even blacker than the blackness of the bedroom night. Pete knew the skeleton was using that blackness inside its skull to look at him. But once again, anxious footsteps were sounding in the hall. Once again, he had woken up his parents—probably Gwen as well.

The skeleton flung out its arms. The shadows in the room moved in as if it had beckoned them, and it vanished. The bedroom door burst open. Someone turned on the light. It was Pete's father this time. And there was Gwen, close behind him.

"Oh, dear!" Pete's father was murmuring. "More bad dreams?"

Pete did not know what to say. If he explained that a skeleton had been dancing and rattling in the moonlight at the foot of his bed, who would believe him? Those bones had been frightening—but impossible. After all, if Gwen had tried to tell him that *she* had seen a ghost dancing under the rib-rafters, he would not have believed her. The horror of it was entirely his own.

"I did have a bit of a dream," he mumbled, and was amazed to hear how his words came panting out. He sounded like a boy who had been running uphill, barely escaping from something savage snapping at his heels.

"That's two nights," said Gwen. "Bad dreams are moving in on you." To his surprise, she actually sounded as if she were sorry for him.

Morning finally came, and with morning came breakfast, which was always reassuring. As he ate some toast, Pete found himself staring at the picture above the fireplace—the picture of that overdressed girl.

"I wonder what her name was," he said.

"I don't know," said Gwen. "I know she died when she was a kid—and I know she died when she was—well, probably soon after that picture was painted."

"Died? How did she die?" asked Pete, looking at the picture with dismay.

"I think she drowned," said Gwen. "She fell into the river, and she was wearing too many clothes to swim in. They weighed her down under the water, and it took people a long time to find her again."

"How do you know?" asked Pete, trying to look at her as if she were tricking him.

"Because I was here with Mom the first time she came here," Gwen said. "And I asked the lady this house belongs to. That picture girl is sort of related to her in some way . . . she was a great-aunt or something . . . and her story belongs to this house."

Pete sighed.

"This house . . ." he repeated, almost like an echo. "I reckon it's a bit doomed, even if it does have velvet cushions and all that stuff."

"It's a *great* house," Gwen cried indignantly, and Pete, who had almost been ready to tell her about the dancing midnight skeleton, fell silent.

That night, when Pete went to his bedroom, he stood for a moment, looking over at the window. Then, with shaky but determined hands, he pulled the curtains open before scrambling into bed. And that night he did not go to sleep but lay awake in the dark, staring toward the slot of window, watching and wincing but determined to work things out. Moonlight began to edge into his room. Pete sighed and swallowed. The moonlight spread a little.

Maybe it was a dream, he thought. *Maybe there's nothing to solve.*

But, as he thought this, he felt the room change around him . . . felt the air somehow thicken, imprisoning him in shadow. And then the skeleton appeared, standing in the shaft of moonlight, holding bony fingers up in the air.

Now! Pete told himself. *Now! Before you have time to be scared!*

"I know who you are!" he said quickly. "You're the girl in the picture over the fireplace." He was only guessing, but as he said this, he suddenly felt sure that he was right.

The skeleton whirled and, as it whirled, it nodded. Moonlight stroked the smooth top of the skull. Amazingly, that thin voice came out of its grinning teeth—that curious, distant, out-of-tune voice struggling to make itself heard.

"You can *see* me," it said. "No one else sees me. They feel me dancing by, but they can't *see* me. You must be special."

"You're the bones—the bones of that girl in the picture, aren't you?" Pete said again, trying to keep his own voice steady. "You're her ghost."

"This was *my* room once," said the ghost. "But I was never allowed to dance back then. I wasn't allowed to sing. My grandmother wanted me to be—to be serious about life, and she was the one in charge of me. Oh, she was a real witch of a grandmother, she was. And this room was my prison."

"I think I'd like this room," said Pete. "Well, I'd like it if I could *sleep* in it. But you come haunting and waking me up with your singing."

"I used to sing in here, but if my grandmother heard me, she'd thump on the door to shut me up. She was sad, so sad, and she wanted me to be sad as well. She thought being happy was not quite respectable."

"Is it—is it strange being a ghost?" Pete asked cautiously. "Is it strange being—being worn down to bones?"

The ghost spun on its toes. Pete thought it might break apart.

"But I *love* being bones," the ghost cried out in its strange voice—that voice without any breath in it. "Back when I was real, in your sort of way, everything I wore was made to tie me in or weigh me down. Even my skin felt like a prison to me." The ghost flung its arms wide. "But bones turned out to be my freedom. Free of tight coats! Free of heavy flesh! Now I can dance . . . dance . . . dance. Now I can sing. And now, at last, at last, I'm truly free. I've been set free by you."

"By me?" Pete asked. "Free?"

"Free!" repeated the ghost voice. "Yes! Free! I have been so tied down by my story . . . tied into this room, that is. I have tried to talk to people . . . tried to sing my story to them . . . but most people can't hear, and the people who can hear won't listen. Bones frighten them. But you—you have listened to me, so now I have told someone—I have told *you*. And suddenly all that heavy past is dissolving. Dissolving! I can feel it. And I am dissolving, too. I'll get beyond being bones. I shall become part of that tree by the window—part of the garden out there. I'll become buds and boughs. I'll have a partner . . . the wind. I'll dance and sing with the wind. People will breathe me in and feel suddenly happy without knowing why."

As she said this, Pete heard wind blowing around the corner of the house, rustling in the leaves of the tree out there, which scraped its branches against the window, so that he looked toward the window for a moment. And when he looked back, the skeleton-ghost was gone. Gone from the room, at any rate. Perhaps she had really broken out at last . . . become part of that tree tapping at the window, part of the summer garden, dancing with the wind . . . there and not-there.

"Funny!" Pete said softly to himself, staring into the empty moonlight. "Funny-strange, that is. Funny-strange to think that being bones might mean you were let loose—turned free to dance and sing. Funny-strange!"

And then he went to sleep and did not wake up until morning, when sunlight pushed into his room, and the tree outside his window tapped at the glass, just as if it were a good friend inviting him out into a new day.

ABOUT THE AUTHORS

Todd Strasser

Todd Strasser is the author of more than 130 books for teens and middle graders, including the Help! I'm Trapped In . . . series, and numerous YA novels, including *The Wave, Give a Boy a Gun, Boot Camp, If I Grow Up,* and his latest, a thriller, *Wish You Were Dead.* His books have been translated into more than a dozen languages, and he has also written for television; for newspapers, such as *The New York Times*; and for magazines, such as *The New Yorker* and *Esquire*. The story "YNK" was inspired by his children, who insisted that he learn how to send and receive text messages.

Help! You're Trapped in Todd Strasser's Body is now at www.toddstrasser.com or at http://toddstrasser.blogspot.com.

David Levithan

David Levithan is more spooked by ghost stories than he is by actual ghosts. He has yet to see a ghost in his own apartment . . . but you never know. If he finds one, he'll let you know on www.davidlevithan.com.

Elizabeth C. Bunce

Elizabeth Bunce has loved ghost stories since her nights huddled under the covers with a flashlight and a book. For this collection, Elizabeth wanted to tell a story about the only spooky thing that ever really gave her the creeps: the hand of glory. This old European legend has been around for hundreds of years, but it first became a charm for thieves in eighteenth-century England. "In for a Penny" is set in the Gold Valley, the imaginary world of Elizabeth's first novel, *A Curse Dark as Gold*. *Curse*, which retells the story of Rumpelstiltskin with a ghostly twist, received the ALA's first William C. Morris YA Debut Award in 2009 and was named a Smithsonian Notable Book for Children.

Elizabeth is hard at work on a new novel, which, like "In for a Penny," is about a thief who finds herself in over her head. She lives near Kansas City, Missouri, with her attorney, her dogs, and a boggart who steals books. Visit her Web site at www.elizabethcbunce.com.

Nina Kiriki Hoffman

Over the past twenty-some years, Nina Kiriki Hoffman has written adult and young-adult novels and more than 250 short stories. Her works have been finalists for the World Fantasy, Mythopoeic, Sturgeon, Philip K. Dick, and Endeavour awards. Her first novel won a Stoker award, and her short story "Trophy Wives" won a 2009 Nebula.

Nina's young-adult novel *Spirits That Walk in Shadow* and short science-fiction novel *Catalyst* came out in 2006. *Fall of Light* was published in May 2009.

Nina does production work for the magazine *Fantasy & Science Fiction*. She also works with teen writers. She lives in Oregon with several cats and many strange toys.

About "Growth Spurt," she says: "I went away to camp for six weeks the summer of my twelfth year, and I did a lot of changing over that summer—some of my clothes didn't fit me by the time I got home. I didn't find a magic answer to help me, unless you count making up stories."

For a list of Nina's publications, check out: http://ofearna.us/books/hoffman.html.

Richard Peck

Richard Peck's newest novel, *A Season of Gifts*, is third in the saga featuring Grandma Dowdel. *A Long Way from Chicago* won the 1999 Newbery silver medal, and *A Year Down Yonder* won the 2001 Newbery gold medal.

Both *A Long Way from Chicago* and his Civil War novel, *The River Between Us*, were National Book Award finalists.

More of his short stories are collected in *Past Perfect, Present Tense*, his 2004 collection that includes "Five Helpful Hints" for writing the short story.

In 2002 he received the National Humanities Medal in a White House ceremony. He has lived in New York City half his life, but his stories tend to drift back to his Midwestern beginnings.

He says about his story: "I was doing research for a novel in which a young character sinks on the battleship *Maine*, and I noticed that it sank the day after Valentine's Day. And that gave me an idea. I looked up and there stood Imogene."

R.L. Stine

Robert Lawrence Stine has sold more than 350 million books in 32 languages, making him the bestselling children's author of the twentieth century.

In 1992, R.L. wrote his first Goosebumps book, *Welcome to Dead House*. He has since written more than one hundred creepy Goosebumps titles—with more to come.

R.L.'s other popular book series include Fear Street, The Nightmare Room, Mostly Ghostly, and Rotten School.

R.L. says he woke up one morning, and the title and idea for "The Three-Eyed Man" popped into his head. "This never happened to me before," he says. "I sat up in bed—and I could SEE the three-eyed man! It was scary! I had to go sketch out the story before I could have breakfast!"

R.L. lives in New York City with his wife, Jane, and King Charles spaniel, Minnie. You can find more scary stories, games, and author info at www.rlstine.com.

Margaret Mahy

Margaret Mahy is nearly seventy-four—an age at which horror stories about bones take on a curious authenticity. But then, she has enjoyed horror stories from an early age. She used to listen whenever possible (for her parents tried to prevent this happening) to a radio serial called *The Phantom Drummer*, which featured a vampire. The fascination with horror tales has continued to entertain her, for they touch on those mysterious and alarming aspects of imaginative possibility implicit in many ancient folktales—tales for the whole human community, which, though it rejoices in happy endings, also needs to have its fearful mysteries acknowledged, too.

Margaret was born (and lives) in New Zealand and is the author of more than 200 stories for children and young adults. She has twice won Britain's Carnegie Medal for Children's Literature and in 2006 was presented with the Hans Christian Andersen Award, which is given to a living author whose works have made a lasting contribution to children's literature. Margaret is not only a writer but a fascinated reader as well, and feels she has been partly created by the stories . . . funny and frightening, gentle and poetic . . . that she has read over the years.

Enjoy the stories in this book! Those are her instructions!

Lois Metzger, Editor

Lois Metzger is the author of several young-adult novels, including *Missing Girls* (a *New York Times* Best Book for Children), and many short stories for anthologies all over the world.

In addition to editing *Bones* and its companion volume, *Bites: Scary Stories to Sink Your Teeth Into*, she has edited three other collections of original short stories for Scholastic—*The Year We Missed My Birthday, Can You Keep a Secret?*, and *Be Careful What You Wish For*. She has also written two nonfiction books—*Yours, Anne: The Life of Anne Frank* and *The Hidden Girl: A True Story of the Holocaust* (with Lola Rein Kaufman).

She lives in New York City with her husband and son.

ACKNOWLEDGMENTS

Special thanks to Gabrielle Balkan, Linda Ferreira, Elizabeth Krych, Janet Kusmierski, Arthur A. Levine, Judy Newman, Andrea Davis Pinkney, and Roy Wandelmaier at Scholastic, and to Susan Cohen, Ellen Datlow, and Lauri Hornik . . .

. . . and to the masterful writers in this book, who know, better than anybody, the thrill of a good scare and how to take you for the ride of your life.

If you liked BONES, you'll love Bites!

Bites

Christopher Paul Curtis • Kevin Emerson • Joshua Gee • Peter Lerangis • Douglas Rees • Neal Shusterman and Terry Black • Ellen Wittlinger • Edited by Lois Metzger

Scary Stories
to Sink Your Teeth Into

SCHOLASTIC

READY FOR **spine-tingling tales**
BY SOME OF TODAY'S BEST WRITERS?
JUST KEEP IN MIND A FEW SIMPLE **warnings:**

SOME **vampires** DON'T WANT JUST YOUR **blood...**
THEY WANT SOMETHING EVEN MORE VALUABLE.

werewolves, ONCE DEAD, DON'T ALWAYS STAY THAT WAY.

SOME DOGS AND COYOTES MAY LOOK NORMAL
—but don't get too close.

Remember...
WHAT YOU DON'T KNOW CAN BITE YOU.

THE SCARIEST PLACE ON EARTH!

EnterHorrorLand.com